BISEXUAL
BUCKAROOS

Seven Bi Group Encounters In
The Tingleverse

Volume 2

CHUCK TINGLE

This moment proves love is real.

- Chuck Tingle

CONTENTS

THE SUN AND THE MOON BANG ME
BISEXUALLY

Astronomy has been my thing for a very long time, well before I even understood or quantified my interest in this field. Years ago, back when I didn't even know what the word meant, I'd gaze up at the stars above and wonder what was out there, thinking all the questions that have been dancing around in the heads of human beings since their initial crawl from the primordial ooze.

How far does the universe go? What is beyond the stars and will we ever get there ourselves? Is there life out there somewhere staring back at us, thinking the same things?

These musings stuck with me, and now that I'm an adult, I've filled a huge amount of my free time with continuing to think on them, staring up into the sky in exactly the same way. Of course, these days I have much better observational equipment, and I also know where to look.

I'm still no closer to any concrete answers, but I enjoy asking the questions even more than ever.

Having this kind of interest while living in the big city is a double-edged sword. On one hand you've got plenty of like-minded amateur astronomers to connect with, and a variety of different clubs to join. Most of these clubs have access to telescopes or other equipment that I could only dream of affording on my own.

The problem, however, is the bright city lights. When I'm gazing out across these buildings from some hillside perch above, it's easy to recognize the man-made beauty as something to behold, but it's nothing when compared to those glittering stars up above. From my apartment, the light pollution makes any star gazing almost impossible.

That's why I'm so excited for this weekend.

"What do you think the big surprise is?" I ask my friend, Heather, from my place in the passenger seat.

She shakes her head, her eyes trained on the road before us as we hurtle deeper and deeper into the desert, far from the land of concrete and cars and lights. Our astronomy group is meeting out here for an overnight trip, which would already be exciting in itself, but there are murmurs of something even more special on the horizon.

"I've really got no idea," Heather offers in return. "I looked up everything I could find on cosmic happenings, and there's nothing all that strange. I mean, we're definitely going to spot a lot of meteors, but meteor showers aren't quite rare enough to get Norm excited."

Norm is the unofficial leader of our group, at least based on experience. Technically speaking, there is no hierarchy here, but Norm is just too damn smart not to end up in that position, whether he wants it or not.

"He was really freaking out at the last meeting," I confirm. "I know Norm's a smart guy, but right now it seems like he might be in over his head. Did you know he's keeping all this a secret? He's not telling anyone else in the field, just our little group. He didn't even post about it online."

"Why?" Heather questions.

"He said he doesn't want a bunch of news reporters out in the desert spoiling our view," I reply.

Heather laughs. Sure, Norm is a certified genius, but the idea of him calculating some kind of astronomical knowledge that *every other scientist on Earth* just happened to miss out on is a bit of a stretch.

I'm tempering my expectations, but I also can't help but imagine the possibilities.

"We'll know soon enough," my friend says as she finally pulls off the freeway and onto a dusty dirt road.

The sun is just about setting over the distant horizon, painting the sky with a blossoming cascade of oranges, purples and reds. It's utterly majestic, and the silhouettes of tall cacti that pass us by only add to the beauty of this glorious scene.

"Wow," is all I can think to say, adrift in a trance as the landscape unfolds before us.

I stay like this for a good while, completely losing track of time until, suddenly, this haze is broken by the car pulling off at a small collection of silver airstream trailers parked in a semi-circle by the side of the road. We're here.

Soon enough, Heather and I are climbing out of the car, greeted with open arms by a handful of other stargazers who are excited to see us.

Norm approaches and gives me a big hug. "Mark, so glad you could make it this weekend!" he offers.

"Well, I kinda had to," I reply once I finally pull back. "You talked it up quite a bit. I'm really curious what you found."

"I *could* spoil it for you," my friend offers temptingly, "but I think you'll be a lot happier if you just see it for yourself."

"Has anyone else taken you up on the offer?" I question, glancing around at our astronomy group.

Norm shakes his head. "Everyone else wanted to wait."

"Sounds like a plan then," I reply.

I leave Norm and head back to the others, who I now see have a fire pit going in the middle of the trailers. Chairs are gathered haphazardly around the flames while others are hard at work preparing dinner and tipping back a few ice-cold chocolate milks. The stars themselves are wonderful, but this kind of warm, inviting atmosphere is another reason I love my astronomy community.

Soon enough, I've pretty much forgotten the mysterious reason Norm dragged us all out here, focused instead on catching up with my friends. The group is a wonderful assortment of people from all walks of life, and their stories fill me with a deep and powerful joy. When the food finally arrives the gathering turns into a feast for both my mind, and my mouth.

Only after the party finishes their dinner does Norm step forward, his face illuminated by the flickering firelight. By now, the sun as disappeared completely, allowing the sky to open up with its vast blackness above. Without a cloud in sight, we have a clear view of everything, even the dust of distant galaxies becoming visible to the naked eye.

"Tonight is a very special night," Norm announces, quieting down the group. "I've made a discovery I think you'll all find very interesting."

My heart starts to beat a little faster now, anxious to hear what's next.

"There's going to be a meet up this evening that very few humans have ever experienced, not because it's so rare, but because they don't know where to look," Norm continues. "However, due to a little investigating on my part, I've discovered the exact location of this astral rendezvous."

I'm trying my best to follow along, to read between the lines of what Norm is saying, but right now I'm having a hell of a time.

"What is it?" someone calls out from the crowd, causing the rest of us to immediately join in with cries of our own.

"Why don't you take a look?" Norm replies with a grin. "Just prepare yourselves. This is a once in a lifetime moment."

With that, Norm turns and heads off into the darkness of the desert. The rest of us exchange confused glances, then one by one begin to climb to our feet and follow along. I blend into the crowd, making my way out to a small hill in the dirt where seven or so telescopes have been set up.

I'm one of the first to arrive, carefully leaning down and putting my eye against the viewer. I can tell that Norm has set up all of these scopes to a precise location, so I do everything I can to avoid disturbing their alignment.

I hold my breath, aching to unravel the mysteries of the sky that have been laid out before me, but upon gazing through the telescope viewer I quickly discover that nothing is there.

"I don't see anything," I report.

"Just wait," Norm continues. "They'll be arriving soon."

Just as he says this, I notice the moon has started to creep its way into the small circle of my viewfinder. I watch as the glowing sphere drifts farther and farther along, enchanted by the presence of the beautiful heavenly body.

Suddenly, I gasp. On the other side of my viewfinder, an equally recognizable presence has emerged. She's sneaking along, just not glowing at her full, glorious blaze that I'm accustomed to. It's the sun.

"There she is!" Norm announces proudly. "The sun and the moon having a secret nightly meeting! For years it was assumed these two celestial objects did not meet at night, only crossing paths in the day time, but now we can see the sun is, in fact, coming back to us under the cover of darkness."

"How did you know?" someone asks in astonishment.

"The other day I heard them exchanging hushed words at the grocery store," Norm explains. "They were talking quietly about a meet up that night."

I continue to stare in amazement, watching as the sun and the moon being to chat each other up. From this far away, I can't make out what either of them are saying, but their body language already displays a deep and powerful attraction to one another.

Of course, who wouldn't be attracted to the sun or the moon. I've always thought the moon was quite handsome, a muscular sphere with chiseled abs and a dark, brooding demeanor. The sun, on the other hand, is bright and cheery, but she's no less attractive. I'd likely catch myself sharing if it weren't for the fact this would do permanent damage to my eyes.

"What are they doing?" I mumble under my breath, gazing intently. "Why not just meet up during the day?"

Suddenly, my question is answered as the sun and the moon embrace, kissing one another passionately. I gasp as I see this, completely taken off guard as the two of them begin to make out.

The whole group erupts in a chorus of shock and awe, blown away by what they're seeing.

It suddenly occurs to me, however, that this moment is a private one. Despite the incredible size of these celestial bodies, they're clearly trying to keep things low key by heading out into the desert like this.

Unless, of course, they *want* a small audience.

My question is quickly answered when the sun turns to look directly a me, locking eye contact through the viewfinder and offering a flirtatious wink.

"What the fuck," I blurt.

The moon turns to look in our direction as well, acknowledging me with a thoughtful nod, then turns back towards the sun as their passionate kissing continues.

"Are you sure it was an accident that you overheard them?" I call over to Norm. "It seems like they want us here."

"Maybe so," the man replies, deep in thought. "Maybe so."

The rest of the group aren't sure what to make of all this, but eventually people start to peel off and head back towards the fire pit.

"This is kinda weird," Heather mumbles. "I mean… I know they're *into* being watched, but I wasn't really prepared for this kind of night."

The rest of the astronomers appear to be on the same page, which is just *wild* to me. They are leaving one by one, but I wouldn't dream of tearing myself away. Clearly the sun and the moon are looking for a small group of voyeurs, and I'm quite happy to be one of them.

I glance over and see that Norm is the only other person left, watching happily as these beautiful floating orbs put on a show.

When I look back through the viewfinder, however, I see that the two have stopped their passionate make out session. They're staring right at us, at *me*. The moon points in my direction and then beckons me towards them.

My heart skips a beat. Is this really happening?

"Are you seeing what I'm seeing?" Norm calls over.

"Yeah, I think so," I stammer in response.

"I think that's for you," Norm continues.

"What do I do?" I question.

Norm considers this for a second. "They're drifting towards the mountaintop over there, if you hurry you can probably make it. There's no road up there but if you start running I bet you could make it in thirty minutes. Just be careful for cacti out there in the desert."

"So I just go... fuck the sun and the moon?" I question.

"Uh... yeah," Norm blurts. "Of course you do."

Realizing how fleeting this moment really is, I spring into action. I take off running into the darkness, my eyes trained sharply on the shapes and shadows that zoom past me in every direction. I'm deeply focused on not running into something sharp or falling and twisting my ankle, but as long as I can avoid these two things, I should be just fine.

Soon enough I've reached the bottom of the hill, then swiftly begin my climb. In other circumstances I'd likely be winded already, but right now I'm too turned on to care. It's as though my arousal has blessed me with some kind of supernatural strength and agility.

Finally, I reach the top of the mount, cresting up over the edge to find the sun and the moon waiting for me.

"Hey," offers the sun seductively. "We didn't know if you'd make it."

"I'm here," is all that I can think to say, my breathing heavy.

"You certainly are," the moon chimes in, his dark eyes looking my body up and down.

I walk towards them slowly, and soon enough the celestial forms are on either side of me, kissing me passionately as they explore my body with their hands.

"Oh my god," I blurt. "I can't believe this is happening."

"It's happening," the sun coos.

The two of them begin to strip away my clothing, undressing me slowly as the cool night air of the desert dances its way across my skin. Soon enough, I'm standing completely naked between them, sandwiched on either side. The astral beings begin to kiss their way down my neck, allowing their attention to gradually drift lower and lower. They reach my shoulders, then my chest, then my abs. The next thing I know, the sun and the moon are hovering at my waistline, teasing me playfully with the prospect of more.

The sun and the moon gaze up at me playfully from below, laughing together as they watch me squirm and ache.

"You want us to suck that fat cock of yours?" the moon questions, his deep, soothing voice sending a chill of arousal through my body.

"Sounds like fun to me," the sun chimes in.

"Yes," I groan. "Please."

"Are you sure?" the sun questions, teasing me.

"I'm sure," I continue.

Finally, the moon relents, opening wide and taking my dick between his lips. The handsome luminous circle begins to pump his head up and down across my length, orally servicing me with expert enthusiasm. He starts slowly at first, working me with a series of graceful pumps while the sun cradles my hanging balls in her hand. The sensation is incredible, and they make a fantastic team as the two of them work diligently together.

Faster and faster the moon goes until finally he pulls back with a gasp, unable to move any quicker. Now the sun scoots into position, a fire in her eyes.

She opens wide and takes my rod between her lips, but her technique is far removed from that of the moon. Instead of bobbing her face up and down, the sun simply draws my rod deeper and deeper into her gullet. Somehow the sun manages to relax her gag reflex, allowing my shaft to slide past and find itself completely consumed. Soon enough, I'm being held in a perfectly performed deep throat, the sun's beautiful face pressed up hard against my abs.

I place my hands on the back of her head, holding her like this for a good while until she finally pulls back with a sputter and a gasp. The suns eyes are wild with carnal excitement, ready for what's next.

"Your turn," I tell her, climbing down onto my knees as she moves back a bit. I crawl towards the sun, opening up her legs and then diving into her warm, flaming pussy.

I begin to flick my tongue rapidly across her clit, moving back and forth in a series of soft, yet quick movements. The sun closes her eyes tight, savoring the sensations that begin to flow through her body.

Meanwhile, the moon climbs into position behind me. I wasn't expecting him, but the first thing I do when I glance back over my shoulder is break into a wide smile. "You like that tight ass?" I question.

The moon nods, giving my rump a playful slap as he aligns his swollen cock with my tightly puckered back door. The enormous sphere teases me for a moment, testing the limits of my anal seal with the head of his cock, then finally pushes forward in a single, deep thrust.

"Oh fuck!" I yelp, not entirely prepared for his incredible size.

The sensation is quite uncomfortable at first, but the moon is a patient lover. His rod firmly planted within my butthole, the lunar globe stays completely still, allowing me a moment to adjust to his enormity.

In the mean time, I turn back to the sun and return to my diligent oral task. I'm applying more pressure now, using my tongue to push her closer and closer to a powerful orgasm.

The longer I work the sun like this, the more I can feel my butthole relaxing. I'm loosening up, and soon enough the moon begins to pump in and out of me. By now, the feelings of discomfort have started to slip away, dissipating slowly as they're replaced by a warm ache of pleasant fullness.

Soon enough, the moon falls into a confident rhythm, hammering away at my ass while I eat out the sun with long, sloppy drags of my tongue. Every slam from behind pushes me against the sun's pussy, and she's clearly loving every second of it.

It's not long before the sun begins to tremble and quake, this celestial form hurtling towards the edge of a powerful climax. Her stomach tenses up, pulling taut as the pressure within her builds. I slip two fingers within, still working her with my tongue until, finally, the sun erupts with a powerful orgasm. I pull back a bit as solar flares blossom across her body, illuminating the scene, but immediately center myself once more and dive back in. I make sure to carry her across the finish line completely, despite the warmth against my face, and fortunately come away without any burns.

Finally, the sun falls back in exhaustion, utterly satisfied.

The moon still hammers away at my ass, pounding me forcefully as my body starts to flood with its own orgasmic sensations. Deep within the pit of my stomach I can feel the warmth beginning to spill out, pulsing through my veins as it works its way across me.

I glance back over my shoulder at the moon, aching for more. "Fuck me!" I demand. "Fuck me harder!"

The moon does as he's told, slamming away at my rump with even more ferocity than before. When I turn back around, I find that the sun is not yet finished, sliding down into position below. She opens her legs wide, aligning her body so that I can easily slip deep into her pussy, which I do with a single gracious thrust.

The feeling of being held between these two astrological giants is almost too much to handle, but I somehow manage to hold back my load from exploding right then and there. Not that this would be such a terrible way to cum, but right now the last thing I want is for this incredible moment to end.

It's not long before the three of us fall into a rhythm together, somehow making this long chain of bisexual insertions work. The pleasure is passing back and forth between us evenly now, and our moans begin to grow louder and louder as they echo out across the desert landscape below.

While this meeting was clearly something of a secret, it's also exciting to know that someone out there is watching and enjoying the show. I've never been one to put myself on display like this, but tonight is clearly a night for trying new things.

I meditate on this for a while, enjoying the pleasant feelings that flow through my body. However, my thoughts are broken when, behind me, the moon begins to moan. He's closing in on the end of his journey, and at this point I'm happy to encourage him.

"Do it!" I demand. "Blow that hot lunar load right up my asshole!"

The moon continues to slam away at me, his groaning escalating until finally he just can't hold back any longer. The enormous floating sphere pushes deep and erupts within, his hot white jizz spilling out in a cascade of pearly liquid. The cum fills me up to the brim, squirting out from the edges of my tightly packed butt and running down the back of my legs in thick, milky streaks.

"Now it's your turn!" the sun cries out, cheering me on as I continue to slam into her.

It's not long before I'm hurtling over the edge of a climax of my own, completely lost in the moment as I throw my head back and let out a long, unbridled howl. My voice echoes out through the night as jizz erupts from the head of my cock, filling up the sun. Every nerve within me is dancing and trembling, experiencing sensations that I'd never dreamed were possible. It's such a potent feeling that I'm lifted up out of my own physical form, looking down on the tangled mess of bodies from above, as though I've momentarily transformed into some kind of astral traveler myself.

When I finally finish, I slam back down into my body, aching and exhausted. I can't remember the last time I felt this satisfied.

"That was amazing," I groan. "Thanks for inviting me up here for your little party."

"You're welcome," offers the sun. "It was our pleasure."

The sun, the moon and I unravel ourselves from one another, then take a seat on the top of the mountain. We gaze out at the endless desert below, lost in thought as we gradually begin to gather our wits.

"Can I ask you both a question?" I continue, breaking the silence.

The sun and moon exchange glances, clearly enchanted by the curiosity of their new human lover. "Go ahead," replies the moon.

"I spend so much time gazing up at the stars and wondering what's beyond, but the view from down here isn't very good. I'm just a tiny little human and you're both these *huge* astral forms drifting through space," I explain. "Now that I've got you here, I've gotta ask… what's out there? What's beyond the stars?"

"Well, you've come to the right place for a question like that, because I'm literally a star," the sun reminds me. "We stars talk a lot, so I've got a pretty good idea about the answer to your question."

"Really?" I blurt. "You do?"

The sun nods. "The question is: do you *really* want to know?"

I consider her words for a moment, not taking this lightly, then finally nod. "Yeah, I do. What's beyond the stars?"

"The edge of the page," the sun informs me bluntly. "It's just the end of the book. After that, there's a whole other world, but this other world is where the reader lives."

"I have no idea what you're talking about," I admit.

"You're a character in a book," the sun states, clear and direct. "We all are."

I glance over at the moon, deeply concerned. He just nods in confirmation.

"I'm just a character in a book?" I repeat back in astonishment, more to myself than anyone else.

The sun laughs. "Not *just* a character in a book. It's a very important role to have. Fictional characters create wonder just like the stars do."

"Really?" I stammer. "They do?"

"That awe you've been chasing your whole life… it's just as much out there as it is in here," the sun offers, pointing to my heart, "and in here."

The sun points to my ass.

"Whoa," a gush, letting the single word fall out of my mouth in excitement. "So what does it mean? What happens now?"

"Now the book ends," the sun continues, "but don't worry. Somebody is bound to open it up again. In fact, if you're here right now it's because someone decided to read us."

"I guess it's not so bad being a fictional character," I admit.

The sun nods. "Nope. It's pretty fun. I'll see you the next time around. Can't wait to meet up again."

BISEXUAL VAMPIRE UNICORNS TEACH ME THE IMPORTANCE OF THE VAMPIRE COUGH

As a health care professional, I can't remember I time when I was more exhausted than this. There've been plenty of moments when my ability to stay focused and alert was tested, late nights at the hospital where I held myself together for hours or even days longer than I expected, but nothing compares to what it's been like dealing with the trotting plague.

The trotting plague is a strange illness that has come on quickly, causing anyone infected to begin a sudden and playful prance, their knees high and their hands out as though they were pretending to be a pony. These trotters feel the compulsion to prance around in this way for an entire day, at which point they tucker out and the symptoms subside. By that time, however, they've already infected a countless number of others who will soon begin a similar trot.

"But *why* does it matter?" some might ask. "They're just trotting playfully around."

It's true, there are worse things than trotting that an illness could compel you to do, but that's exactly the point. Trotting is a pure and playful activity, something that should never be done through the force of a foreign influence.

In the name of all that is good in this world, Buck Tangle will stand up and fight for the sanctity of a wholesome, decent trot.

It's that kind of commitment to helping others that drove me to being a doctor in the first place. I'm not just *any* doctor either, I'm one of the hard working medical practitioners who has specifically positioned themselves to help out in an outbreak such as this.

Half my time is spent on the ground floor of it all, treating patients and making sure they're getting the proper care they deserve, and the other half is dedicated to finding ways of stopping these illnesses at their source. I've been staying after hours in the lab, trying to come up with any solution that I can while the world spins on in chaos around me. When I find even the slightest shred of an answer, I pass it along and let this information flow out into the world, hopefully creating policies that could make others just a little bit safer.

Washing your hands? That was me.

Staying inside and social distancing? I came up with that, too.

Now, however, I'm at a loss. It appears I've given all the advice that I possibly can, and now there's nothing else I can do to help slow this exponential outbreak.

Of course, self-quarantining and social distancing is the best thing people can do right now, but what if they absolutely *have* to leave the house to see a doctor? How should they behave in the waiting room? Or what if they share a house with someone who isn't sick yet, and there's simply not enough space to keep the two people safely apart?

There *must* be more strategies left, some untapped resource that can be scoured for helpful information.

"Hey Dr. Tangle, what are you still doing here?" a voice cuts through the darkness behind me.

I turn around in the dim light of my lab to see my friend and co-worker, Bossica Tream, standing in the doorway.

"Just doing a little more research," I inform her, turning away from my microscope. "There's still a few avenues to test. I think if I separate the protein from the trotting plague virus, I can probably isolate some of the factors that drive the high kicks. It's not the whole prance, but it's something."

Dr. Tream just stares at me blankly, trying to choose her expression with care. I can tell there's something on her mind, something she's dying to get out.

"You should go home," my friend finally says, cracking. "You've been here twice as long as anyone else. You're exhausted."

"I know," I counter, then shake my head, "but I can't. We've gotta get to the bottom of this, people are out there trotting for hours."

Dr. Tream nods with understanding, then tries another approach. "Listen, I know you really want to help, and so far you've done an amazing job. At a certain point, though, you're gonna be too tired to be productive here. You've technically been off the clock for a while now, and that means it's time to get some rest. Take care of yourself."

"They need me," I reply, stubbornly.

"Hank, they need you thinking clear and awake," Jessica reminds me.

She's right, and I know it. Sometimes it can feel like the best course of action is just plowing forward, regardless of the internal cost, but it's rarely the correct move in the long run. If we're gonna make it through this thing they we need to stay focused, and sometimes staying focused means giving yourself a break.

"Take the night off," Dr. Tream says directly. "Get some rest."

I nod in begrudging acceptance. "You're right."

Bossica smiles and then leaves, letting the door drift closed behind her.

Moments later I'm left in the dark silence of my lab once again, meditating on my next course of action. After a while, I force myself to tear away from the equipment, grabbing my coat and pulling it on.

I'm about to head out the door when something stops me in my tracks: a faint glowing light from the back room. Of course, this glow isn't unusual, but as a man of science I rarely pay it much attention.

Here at the hospital, we have many tools that we use in our daily quest for knowledge. It's important that all of them adhere to a scientific guideline in order to produce the best possible results, leaving some mysterious, otherworldly things that go untouched.

I have one such item here in my lab, and ancient tome of knowledge that sits on a dusty shelf next to my medical journals. It's been said that gazing upon the words within can bend the mind of any who seek their cosmic knowledge, but I think that's a bit of an exaggeration.

The book is not *evil,* it's just old and magic. It also kind of scares me.

Still, if there was any time to take a look inside, it would be now. After all, I've tried everything I can manage to get the trotting plague under control. Maybe there's some untapped resource still waiting for me in this ancient book.

I turn and creep back through my lab, heading into the other room and allowing my eyes to look upon the strange glowing volume that sits on my shelf. I pull it off slowly, then open it up, my pupils shifting from the luminous glow.

The language is old and strange, but I can make out the basic points. As I hold the book in my hand, it begins to flip from page to page as though blown by some mystical wind.

Eventually, the book lands on a page with a drawing of an ancient castle, the terrifying building spiraling up towards the sky above in a mass of twisting stone towers.

"Vampire," I read aloud.

Unfortunately, it's too difficult for me to translate the rest.

I close the book, realizing exactly what I have to do. There's a vampire castle about an hour north from here, and while I'd always driven by the place with a healthy dose of fear and caution, I know now that it's exactly where I need to go for the answers I'm looking for.

An excitement in my step, I turn and head out of the lab, grabbing a few trotting plague tests as I go. I've been doing everything I can to not venture out into this harsh new world, but at least I'll be able to test myself and not drag anyone else into this mess should I happen to be infected.

I'm thankful to find that the results of my trotting plague test are negative, but any good will and glee immediately melts away as I pull up to the front gates of this enormous castle. I gaze at the massive structure perched atop this hillside, noting that there seems to be a permanent assortment of storm clouds clustered around it. Lightening flashes twice in the distance, and moments later a pair of cacophonous, thundering booms erupt in my ears.

The gate itself is made of iron and hanging haphazardly from it's rusty hinge, swaying back and forth in the wind. There's plenty of room for me to drive past, and that's exactly what I do as my heart continues to slam hard within my chest. It suddenly hits me that this is probably an incredibly bad idea, that just because some ancient glowing book told me I might find health tips at the vampire castle, I probably shouldn't be headed up here without telling anywhere where I'm going.

In this moment, a powerful wave of caution and regret washes over me. Maybe I should turn around and head back home.

The next thing I know, however, I've already arrived, pulling up to the front of this ancient castle and putting my car in park. The rain is pouring down hard, but the front door features an enormous overhang that will keep me dry should I decide to go through with this.

I take a deep breath and let it out slowly, then finally make my choice. Without another moment of hesitation, I throw open my car door and run up the castle steps, continuing to barrel onward until I find myself somewhere dry.

I wipe the rain away and then rap on the enormous entryway of this castle three times, the iron knocker ringing out with endless hollow booms within.

I wait, then wait some more, eventually considering that the vampiric rumors could be nothing more than gossip and lies. For all I know, this castle could've been abandoned for years.

I begin to turn and walk away, but suddenly stop. The door cracks open and gradually swings wide with a long, loud creak.

"Why, hello there!" comes the a deep and confident Transylvanian accent.

The next thing I know, two figures are standing before me. One is a unicorn with a dark black mane and a flowing cloak of shadows around him. He is tall and breathtakingly handsome, with eyes like coals that scare out at me from his shadowy surroundings.

Next to this unicorn is a second horned creature, ravishing and beautiful in a cloak of her own. Her fabric is red, however, and it matches the stark crimson of her lips.

"Hi," I stammer, trying to regain my composure in the presence of these gorgeous gothic unicorns.

We stand in silence for a moment, and at first I can't tell why until, suddenly, I'm hit with the realization that it's my job to explain my reason for arriving on their doorstep unannounced.

"Oh, sorry," I continue, struggling to collect my thoughts. "I'm Dr. Buck Tangle, and I'm wondering if you could help me with something very important."

The two unicorns exchange glances knowingly, although I can't quite get the meaning of their expression.

"I'm Count Rimble," the unicorn in black replies, finally turning back to face me.

"And I'm Countess Gorba," offers the woman with a sly grin. "You may continue."

"I have this ancient tome of knowledge," I explain, stumbling over my words. "It's this big spooky book, I should've brought it with me but I left it in my car… anyway, this book glows green and it talks to me sometimes. I think it might be twisting my dreams. I don't know… it said I should come see you."

"See us?" Count Rimble questions, "but why?"

"Because it told me to find some vampires," I continue, awkwardly quieting down as I reach the end of my sentence. By the time I've arrived at the final, and most important, word, I'm barely audible.

"What was that?" Count Rimble questions, leaning in a bit.

"Oh," I blurt, awkwardly scratching the back of my neck. "It said I needed to find some vampires."

The unicorns suddenly erupt in a fit of laugher, rolling their eyes at the grand silliness of it all. Eventually, I start to laugh, too, a wave of relief washing over me. Talking to a couple of beautiful unicorns is *much* less frightening then talking to a couple of beautiful unicorn vampires.

"Crazy, right?" I chuckle. "I knew it was silly. There's no such thing as vampires."

"Oh no, we're vampires," Countess Gorba counters. "We were just laughing because you *found our book*. We must've left that at the hospital ages ago!"

"I probably dropped it back when I had my five century physical," Count Rimble adds.

"Wait, so you *are* vampires?" I question, immediately frightened again.

"Yes, but you've got nothing to worry about," Count Rimble continues. "Don't worry, we don't such blood. Only cock."

The unicorn vampires erupt in another fit of laugher.

"Do you want to come in?" Countess Gorba questions, stepping to the side and waving me onward.

"I… don't know," I stammer.

"The sucking off is up to you, obviously, but I think we can help you with that health tip you're looking for," she offers.

It's now or never, and this is exactly the advice I was hoping to receive. Being around vampires is a little stressful, but they seem kind enough, and if they can help me curb the spread of the trotting plague in even the slightest amount, it will all be worth it.

"Before I come in," I suddenly blurt. "You haven't been exposed to the trotting plague, have you? I just tested myself on the way up here and

I'm fine, but I should probably make sure we keep our distance."

"Trotting plague?" Count Rimble asks with a chuckle. "We've been in self-quarantine since the *plague* plague. We never leave!"

With that out of the way, I step inside. The door closes behind me and seconds later the entire living room erupts in a cascade of candlelight. There are melted wax stumps everywhere, lining the shelves and clustered upon the chandelier above. Each and every one of them flickers to life at the same time, as though through the use of some magic spell. A fireplace also roars to life, surrounded by an assortment of red velvet chairs.

"So let's get this health technique out of the way," Countess Gorba offers, then motions towards a nearby seat.

I follow her lead, taking my place in one of the soft chairs and watching as her and her husband stand before me.

"This is called the vampire cough," Countess Gorba begins. "It's an ancient technique, passed down from generation to generation. It will help fight the spread of many diseases, not just the trotting plague. I'll demonstrate."

The countess pulls her arm back, wrapping her cloak around her face in a traditional vampire pose, then coughs loudly into her arm.

"See," the countess continues after pulling away. "Instead of just coughing without covering your mouth, you put your arm in front of it, like a vampire."

It's so simple, yet so elegant. I've been in the medical practice for years and never once considered such a thing.

"You… cover your mouth when you cough?" I question.

"That's right," Countess Gorba and Count Rimble reply in unison.

"What an incredible trick," I continue, then try it myself. I pull my arm back in a vampire pose and then cough into it, amazed at how much I've blocked the spread of tiny particles that would otherwise erupt from my mouth after such a thing.

"Now, this is *only one part* of the process," Countess Gorba continues. "If there's a plague and you're coughing then *you shouldn't be leaving the house*. At all. However, there are a few rare times that you might need to leave, maybe to go to the hospital for treatment, or if you happen to share your home with other people who you don't want to get sick. To be clear: the best option during a plague is to *stay home*. The vampire cough is a little something extra. Also, wash your hands."

"Understood," I reply, nodding in a state of thankful happiness regarding this important new information. "I'm the doctor who came up with that, believe it or not."

"I don't believe it," Countess Gorba replies flatly.

The three of us sit in silence for a moment as the fire flickers and dances, casting brilliant moving shadows across our faces and the nearby stone walls. There's a heavy weight to this moment, something we're all thinking but nobody wants to say out loud.

I have to admit, these unicorn vampires are incredibly sexy. I find myself equally attracted to them in a way that simply can't be denied.

"Would you like to leave now?" Count Rimble finally offers, motioning toward the door.

I shake my head. "You two have been cooped up here for a while," I stammer, my voice trembling a bit. "After giving me such good treatment advice, I feel like there's something I should be giving you in return."

"We are rather hungry," the count continues, "for cock."

The two unicorn vampires approach slowly, every step they take causing my heart to race even faster. Soon enough, they drop down to the floor, crawling their way towards me.

When Count Rimble and Countess Gorba arrive, the two of them reach up and begin to unbuckle my belt. They gaze at me with eyes that overflow with an ancient, aching hunger.

Soon enough, the vampire unicorns are pulling forth my swollen cock from its fabric prison, gasping loudly when confronted by my impressive size.

"What a meal," Countess Gorba offers playfully.

"Ladies first," Court Rimble replies.

The next thing I know, Countess Gorba is opening wide and taking my rock hard dick between her lips. She begins to pump her head up and down across my length, taking her time with me as her husband cradles my balls with his cool vampire hands.

I begin to rock my hips in time with Countess Gorba's movements, the two of us quickly falling into sync with one another as a long, satisfied groan slips out from between my lips. She definitely knows what she's doing, and although the scrape of her long fangs across my shaft gives me pause, she's careful not to stick me with them.

After a good while of this, Countess Gorba finally pulls back with a gasp, allowing her husband to have a turn. Count Rimble quickly takes his position in front of me, opening wide and then swallowing my dick. His technique, however, is quite a bit different than the unicorn countess who came before him.

Instead of bobbing up and down, Count Rimble takes me deeper and deeper within his throat, my rod sliding much further into his gullet that I'd ever expect. The vampire somehow relaxes his gag reflex and allows me passage beyond, my dick plummeting into his absolute depths in a stunningly performed deep throat.

The vampire unicorn holds me here for what seems like forever, allowing me time to savor this feeling of being full consumed. The sensation is incredible, but eventually Count Rimble is forced to pull back with a gasp, spit dangling in a long translucent thread that connects his lips to the head of my shaft.

"Fuck me," I demand. "Pound me right now."

Without another word, I stand up and strip away the rest of my clothing, tossing it to the side. Once I'm completely nude, I climb drop down onto the rug below me, the warmth of the fireplace feeling incredible as it radiates across my bare body. I pop my ass out towards the vampire unicorns behind me, wiggling my rump from side to side and then reacting back to give myself a playful slap.

"What are you waiting for? I coo.

Without hesitation, Count Rimble climbs down into position behind me. "I vant to pound your butt!" he exclaims in his thick accent.

The vampire unicorn teases my backdoor for a moment with his enormous undead cock, testing the limits of my anal tightness and then finally plunging into me with a deep and powerful thrust. I let out a started gasp as he impales my body, not entirely prepared for his girth. My hands grip tight against the rug below, bracing for the vampire unicorn's weight.

Count Rimble is utterly enormous, but he's a patient lover, taking his time with me. The vampire unicorn starts slowly at first, gradually gaining speed as my body relaxes and we fall into a rhythm together. It's not long before we're perfect sync, the sensations of carnal bliss passing back and forth between us.

"Oh fuck, oh fuck, oh fuck," I start to repeat over and over again, the words falling out of my mouth in a hazy mantra as Count Rimble continues to massage my prostate from within. Every passing round the words grows louder and louder until, eventually, I'm crying out at the top of my lungs, completely lost in the moment. "Oh fuck! Oh fuck! Oh fuck!"

I'm in such a potent trance that I don't even notice the beautiful countess climbing down into position before me. Suddenly, however, I discover that the gorgeous vampire unicorn has dropped into the doggystyle position as well, her ass backed up against me as she waits for an insertion of her own.

Count Rimble and I slow down for a moment, hungrily eyeing up the beautiful unicorn.

"Come on," Countess Gorba coos seductively, offering up a wink. "Don't leave me out of this."

I smile wide as she backs all the way up against me, the three of us now creating a long chain of sensuality. The beautiful vampire unicorn reaches back and takes my cock into her hand, aligning my shaft with her pussy and then sighing loudly as she slams back against me.

I slip deep inside her, appreciating the pleasant tightness as all three of our bodies begin to rock together. It takes a little longer than before to find a rhythm, as there is now one more cog in the machine, but eventually we fall into a pulse that works.

The next thing I know, we're all hammering against one another, our moans and groans filling the room and bouncing off the high stone ceilings above. The sensations are passing back and forth between us now with such potent efficiency that I'm not sure where I end and they begin. All that I can feel is a radiant ball of pleasure completely overwhelming me from the inside out.

"I'm gonna fucking cum," the unicorn vampire behind me cries out, elevating the speed of his hammering cock even more. He's giving it to me with everything he's got now, slamming into my asshole with the grace of a unicorn and the strength of a vampire.

Suddenly, Count Rimble thrusts deep within me and holds. I can feel his enormous rod blasting payload after payload of hot white jizz into my rectum, filling me up to the brim until his seed comes squirting out from the edges of my tightly plugged asshole. The cum runs down the back of my legs in long thick streaks, spilling everywhere.

It appears Countess Gorba is on a similar timeline, because the next thing I know she's cumming hard as well. The beautiful vampire unicorn throws her head back and lets out a frantic scream as powerful orgasmic spasms erupt through her body, the pleasure almost too much for her to bear. She's lost in the moment, the muscles across her body tensing and releasing in unison until she finally collapses onto the rug in exhaustion.

"Feed us," the two unicorn vampires begin to groan, pushing me back up to my feet while they remain sprawled out on the floor below.

The two of them are beating me off in tandem, their hands working my shaft and balls with expert precision as the erotic tension builds. Soon enough, the pressure is simply too much for me to maintain, and the next thing I know I'm blasting forth with pump after pump of hot cum. My jizz splatters down across the vampire unicorns, who gobble it up hungrily.

The three of us eventually find ourselves sitting around by the fire, freshly cleaned off from one of the glorious castle showers, and wrapped in warm robes. I don't have time to stay long, however, I need to return to my duties as a doctor.

"I just don't know how I'm going to do it," I explain. "There's a limited amount of patients that I can see in a single day, and I have to get this information out there. Social distancing, self-quarantining, hand washing, the vampire cough: these are ideas that need to be spread."

"Maybe you could write some books about them?" Count Rimble suggests. "That's a good way of getting information out into the world."

I literally gasp when I hear this elegant solution. He's right, I've been thinking way too small. If I want to deliver this information to the masses then I can't just tell them one by one, I've gotta write a book.

"You know what else you should do," Countess Gorba offers. "Throw some sex in. Sex sells. People will come for the fucking, but they'll take away a very important message."

"I love it," I reply, nodding excitedly. "I'll call one of them *Bisexual Unicorn Vampires Teach Me The Importance Of The Vampire Cough.*"

BISEXUAL ARCADE MACHINES WORK MY SLOT

I've been playing videogames since I can remember, starting off in the early nineties when I was just barely old enough to walk. As the motor skills needed to keep me standing upright developed, so did my hand eye coordination. I'd watch as my parents bounced colorful pixels across the screen of our living room television, pulsing lo-fi music erupting out from the speakers and overwhelming my senses as I smiled wide.

Eventually, they started letting me play, and were amazed at how good I was. Soon enough, I was taking my folks down with ease whenever a two-player game was plugged in, an even more amazing feat when you consider the age disparity between us.

Of course, there was plenty of discussion regarding the theory that if I sat in front of the television too long I'd rot my brain. Fair enough, I guess. In those days they'd *joke* about the idea of competitive gaming, and look at the way things turned out.

Fortunately, my parents me keep playing, recognizing that I had a natural skill and it made me happy. As long as I kept an even balance with the rest of my life, it was fine to blow off a little steam behind a joystick.

This balance started to come when I grew old enough to visit the local video arcade down the street from my house. It was close enough to walk, and packed full of all the latest games that you couldn't get on any home consoles. Of course, my parents didn't give a damn about the game variety, they just liked the fact that I was getting out of the house and socializing with other kids.

Truth be told, it's within the walls of that little arcade that I made most of my closest friends. I have wonderful memories of that place, and they've stuck with me all the way up until today.

It shaped me into the person I've become, and brought me to this exact moment as I stand before the glowing screen of an arcade cabinet. I'm no longer in that little spot down the street, in fact, I'm not even in the same state.

"You've got this," my friend Frankie offers, stepping up next to me. "You're so close to this months high score, you can't give up now."

I turn to look at my friend, but I don't say a word. I'm still struggling to sort out my feelings and understand what exactly this moment of disinterest means.

"You need some coins?" Frankie questions, pulling a handful of quarters out of her pocket.

I shake my head, still in a state of disbelief. "I think... I think I'm bored," I finally say.

Frankie's eyes go wide. "Really? You love the arcade."

I nod. "Yeah, I just... I don't really care about getting the high score on Space Raptors right now," I explain, struggling to understand the emotions that swirl within me.

"Let's go grab a bite," Frankie replies.

I accept her offer and the two of us leave the standing arcade cabinet behind, turning around and weaving our way back through the small room. Digital bells and whistles are going off left and right as flashes of neon light erupt across our faces in the dimly lit room. Typically, this would send my heart fluttering, but I still can't seem to care.

The other end of this arcade features a bar, where Frankie and I stop to make our order. I decide on a chocolate milk and a burger, and my friend gets the same. We take our number and head over to a nearby booth, then slide in across from one another.

"So what's up, Bailey?" Frankie questions. "I've known you long enough to know when you're upset about something. Did you lose your job? Sidelined by a breakup? What's going on?"

I shake my head. "Nothing like that. Actually, life is pretty damn good."

"You're the best player that I know, especially on this classic stuff," Frankie continues.

I smile. "Well, thank you. Maybe that's the problem, though. I've been playing all these games for years and now I'm too good at them. I think I'm getting bored."

"They reset the high scores every month," my friend reminds me.

"I know," I continue, "but I'll just beat them again. It's not that hard. When you came up to tell me I could beat the high score if I gave it another shot, I wasn't upset because I disagreed. I was upset because you're right."

Frankie finally understands, nodding along with me. Moments later our meals arrive, fresh from the kitchen and wafting across our nostrils with a glorious, savory scent. We each receive a tall glass of chocolate milk, too, hoisting them up and clinking them together before taking a long sip.

"I guess I'm just bored with these games," I finally say.

A smile slowly begins to make its way across Frankie's face. "I think I've got an idea then," she replies.

"Oh yeah?" I question, taking a huge bite of my burger and chewing happily as I wait for her to continue.

"Have you heard of The Tinglecade?" she questions.

I shake my head.

"Honestly, I'm not even sure if it's real, but I've heard people talking about the place for ages. It's an arcade up in the hills that's super exclusive. They've got all the rarest games; special editions, prototypes, you name it," Frankie explains. "I've heard there's even a copy of Tingle Fighter up there."

My eyes go wide. Tingle Fighter is a legendary arcade cabinet based on the words of the mysterious Dr. Chuck Tingle, an erotica author who specializes in stories about bigfeet, dinosaurs, unicorns and living objects. There are only rumors of its existence, but I never once considered the fact that this rare and highly sought-after game might actually be real.

I suddenly find myself flooded with an excitement that's been sorely missing. I feel like I did when I was young, walking down the street to the local arcade with a pocket full of quarters and a spring in my step.

"How do I find this place?" I question.

Frankie glances back and forth over her shoulders and then leans in close, lowering her voice a bit. "It's at the top of Billings Drive," she explains. "The house with the red door."

"Why haven't you ever gone?" I question.

Frankie shakes her head. "I'm not good enough," she confesses. "They make you play a game before they let you in."

"What game?" I question.

"I don't know," my friend admits, "but I've heard it's tough."

My eyes dart from building to building as I gaze up through the windshield of my car, struggling to spot this notorious red door. Unfortunately, the houses in this neck of the woods are all enormous mansions perched up high, and beyond their overgrown gates it's hard to get a look at much of anything.

I reach the very top of Billings drive and pull over, suddenly wondering if all this is nothing but an urban legend or even a practical joke. Of course, Frankie would never do that to me, but having never gone herself, maybe she's the original target for this little prank.

I let out a long sigh and turn off the engine, climbing out of my car to get a better look. It's late in the evening, and the dying light of the sun doesn't make matters any better. I begin to slowly walk up and down the sidewalk, struggling to see anything past the enormous fences that tower over me.

Eventually, I let out a long, defeated sigh. I begin to turn around and head back to the car when something catches my eye, a strange collection of symbols etched beautifully into one of the iron gates. To most people, these arrows and letters would mean nothing, but I recognize them immediately as the Tinglenami Code, a classic gaming cheat that would unlock various special abilities on older games.

This is the place.

I walk up to the gate and investigate further, discovering it's cracked open slightly. Not knowing what else to do, I slip inside and find myself in a long, overgrown driveway that leads up the mansion. I continue onward, my heart racing now.

"Hello?" I call out.

There's no response.

Eventually, I arrive at the bright red front door of the manor. I knock.

A small metal slot in the middle of the door slides open with a clang. A flat object pops out and then unfolds with a series of mechanical whirs and buzzes, eventually revealing itself to be a video screen. Below it, a controller extends towards my hands.

"Press start," a robotic voice commands.

I press the start button and immediately find myself greeted with a game that I recognize immediately. It's Space Raptor, the exact same game that I'd been playing back at the arcade when this whole adventure started.

I guess it's finally my chance to get the high score.

The game begins and I immediately fall into the usual rhythm, my tiny pixelated space raptor gobbling up as many butts as I can find. The digital scoreboard at the top of the screen quickly begins to roll over, adding up my bonuses as I continue to rack up the points and complete objectives.

Soon enough, I've completely forgotten why I'm here, lost in the game.

When the screen shuts off, I jump back in alarm. "Hey! I was just getting started!" I yell.

"You have completed the high score process," the robotic voice informs me. "You may now enter."

The screen and controller slide back into the door, and moments later there's another loud metallic clang as it begins to swing open.

I push inward and gasp aloud as I see the massive foyer before me. The atmosphere has completely changed, and it's unlike any arcade I've ever been to. Sure, there are videogame cabinets scattered everywhere, but that's where the similarities end.

I'm standing now in a giant, two-story entry way with a curved staircase leading up the walls on either side of me. Everyone here is wearing a finely tailored suit or a fancy dark dress, and they're sipping chocolate milk from ornate flutes or martini glasses. Most of the patrons are wearing black masquerade masks, and soft jazz music tumbles out across the scene to add an air of mystery.

I try my best to act natural as I continue inside, grabbing one of the chocolate milk glasses from a tray when a masked waiter carries it by.

"You're new here," a voice states, causing me to tense up slightly.

I turn to see an arcade cabinet standing next to me, the sensual voice emanating from deep within. Popping out from the screen is the face of a beautiful woman, who smiles mischievously.

"I am," I stammer. "I heard there were some hard to find games here."

The arcade cabinet laughs. "I guess you could say that, it depends on what you're looking for. I'm Jessica." The machine extends a hand, which I shake firmly.

"Bailey," I reply.

"Well, Bailey," the sentient arcade game continues. "What *are* you looking for?"

I consider her question for a moment. "A first edition Bigfoot Pirate Ghostship without the kill screen would be amazing. I would also love to play Billionaire Jetplane Cardshark 2000."

The arcade cabinet immediately starts laughing, clearly aware of something that I'm not.

"What?" I blurt. "Too rare? I was told this place had everything."

"I just don't think you understand where you are," she continues. "I don't think you understand *what this is.*"

"It's an arcade, right?" I counter, confused.

The cabinet puts her arm around me and the two of us begin to walk deeper into the manor. "I suppose so," she replies, "but it's a lot more than that."

As the two of us walk, I begin to notice that many of the humans and arcade machines are not actually involved in any kind of gaming. No high scores are being won here. Instead, these partygoers are chatting it up and getting awfully close to one another. Everyone is certainly having a great time, but not quite in the way I expected.

Soon enough, we come to a set of double doors. Jessica stops here and smiles. "After you," she offers, motioning me onward.

I push through the doors and my eyes go wide as I bear witness to the erotic scene before me. This room is large and round, with cushions and pillows everywhere. Lying across them in a variety of explicit poses are gatherings of humans and arcade cabinets, the groups moaning and groaning in ecstasy as they pleasure one another. The scene is incredible, and while this blatant hedonism is a little startling at first, frightening even, I quickly find myself getting more and more turned on.

I simply can't tear my eyes away. I watch as every imaginable combination of human and machine goes at it, completely lost in the moment.

"Yeah," I finally offer, the word falling limply from my mouth. "Not the kind of party I was expecting at all, but... I like it."

I glance over at Jessica, who raises her eyebrows. "Oh yeah?" the sentient arcade game questions.

The erotic tension surges between us in this moment, lifting it up from the subconscious realm and making our current situation undeniable. Since the second I met Jessica, I'd thought she was incredibly cute, but given the circumstances I didn't think anything could come of it.

Now the circumstances have changed.

"Yeah," I reply with a nod, accepting the arousal that flows through me and making it my own. This place is mysterious and intimidating, but I've conquered enough mad scientists and evil wizards in my day. Something tells me I can handle this high-profile arcade cabinet orgy.

Jessica takes me be the hand and the next thing I know she's leading me deeper into the manor, weaving up and down various hallways and past an assortment of open doors. I sneak glances within these erotic chambers as we go, catching visual flashes of even more couplings as they enjoy themselves in fits of unbridled passion. Eventually, we arrive at a room of our own, stumbling inside as the two of us erupt in a flurry of kisses.

I immediately begin to explore her body, my hands working their way across the hard surface of her semi-rectangular arcade cabinet form. I've enjoyed plenty of games before, but never quite like this.

Jessica explores me with the same level of interest, slowly removing my clothes and exposing my body to the warm air of the mansion. I feel tense at first, but somehow manage to relax as she goes, giving in to the moment. Soon enough, my clothes are lying in a pile on the floor as I stand completely nude before Jessica, still kissing and caressing her form.

"I want you so bad," I groan, the words falling out of my mouth softly.

"You want to play with me?" the arcade cabinet questions.

I nod.

"What else do you want?" she continues.

My eyes are open at this point, and while I continue to kiss the beautiful machine I'm also gazing past her. My attention has fallen onto another arcade game that stands in the hallway, chatting away the evening with someone else. He hasn't noticed me or Jessica, but I've certainly noticed him.

Jessica pulls back, noticing now that I'm distracted. She turned to follow my gaze, then smiles knowing when she sees what I'm looking at.

"Henry?" Jessica questions.

"What?" I blurt, not quite sure what she's asking.

"Is that what you want?" Jessica continues, repeating her query from before.

Suddenly, the pieces all fall into place. In most situations I'd deny my attraction and immediately get back to work focusing on Jessica, but this isn't like most situations.

"Yeah," I finally admit.

"I know him," the arcade cabinet informs me, then turns back towards the hallway. "Hey!" Jessica calls out, catching the attention this handsome arcade machine. "Get over here!"

Henry looks a little confused at first, then smiles warmly when he realizes what's going on. He excuses himself from his current conversation then strolls over to us, closing the door behind him as he enters.

"What's going on in here?" the machine questions, his handsome chiseled face grinning mischievously.

"What does it look like?" Jessica replies, then begins to kiss Henry deeply on the lips.

I sit back for a moment and watch the two machines make out like this, admiring just how gorgeous these classic arcade games really are.

Eventually, though, they pull me back in to the fray. Soon enough, all three of us are kissing, moving our attention back and forth in every combination imaginable.

I drop down to my knees before the machines, gazing up at them with lustful eyes. I see now that neither of them is equipped with a traditional coin slot for inserting quarters. Instead, Jessica has a beautiful, slick pussy, and Henry sports his enormous, rock hard cock.

I have trouble deciding where to start, so I begin by warming them both up with each hand. I rub Jessica's arcade cabinet clit with soft, delicate circles while I take Henry's rod in my other hand, gracefully stroking him off. This particular maneuver is difficult at first, like rubbing your belly and patting your head at the same time, but I somehow fall into it. The two gorgeous vintage arcade machines begin to moan and groan above me, clearly enjoying themselves.

Eventually, I open wide and turn my attention to Henry completely, taking his giant cock between my lips. I pump my head slowly up and down across his length, cradling his hanging balls while I work him. Meanwhile, Jessica continues to kiss and caress his body, only adding to the glorious sensations.

When I can't pump my head across his length any faster, I finally pull back with a frantic gasp. I take a moment to collect myself, then dive back in once again. This time, however, I'm aiming for a completely different technique. Instead of pumping my face over Henry's cock, I push my head farther and farther down onto him.

I continue taking the arcade machine's rod deeper within me, sliding his member all the way down until he reaches the absolute depths of my throat. I've somehow relaxed my gag reflex enough to accept him all the way, and it's here that I allow him to rest in a stunning deep throat.

"Oh fuck," Henry groans, satisfied with this oral maneuver.

Eventually, I pull back, wild eyed and ready for more. I turn my attention to Jessica, diving in and getting to work on her wet arcade cabinet pussy. I start by licking her at the same pace as my fingers, gently tickling her aching clit with my tongue, then eventually build into a steady lap.

Jessica is loving this, enjoying the sensation so much that she begins to stumble, then finally decides to make her way to the ground. The arcade cabinet tips over slowly until she comes to rest on her back. I climb up over her and continue to lick her pussy, furiously working her as she trembles and quakes.

"Fuck yes, work that slot, work that slot," the video game groans, her eyes rolling back into her head.

"What about *my* coin slot?" I question, turning around and looking back over my shoulder at Henry.

The arcade machine gives me a wink and then slides into position behind me, aligning his mammoth cock with my aching pussy.

"Please," I gush. "I need that joystick."

"Player two has joined the game," Henry offers, then pushes into me with a single deep thrust, a movement that causes me to gasp aloud at the game's sheer size. I'd already taken his rod between my lips, so I should've been more prepared for this moment, but I have to admit I'm taken off guard by his formidable size.

Fortunately, Henry is a patient and giving lover, taking his time with me and starting slowly at first. He holds deep within my body as I adjust to his size, then gradually falls into a steady grind against my backside. I push back against him, falling into sync as the two of us move together and the pleasure passes back and forth between us.

Meanwhile, I continue to service Jessica. I frantically lap away at her pussy, keeping up the pace but also adding two fingers to the mix. As I slip them within her arcade cabinet body the machine lets out a soft groan, clearly enjoying the added stimulation.

"Just like that, just like that," she begins to pant, the words falling out of her mouth over and over again in a steady rhythm. She grows louder and louder with every round, until eventually she's screaming out at the top of her lungs. "Just like that! Just like that!"

Her voice begins to distort and change, becoming slightly more robotic as she hurtles towards the edge of orgasm. These vintage machines aren't quite built for this kind of stimulation, but she holds on tight as the two of us continue towards the point of no return together.

Suddenly, Jessica erupts in a wild scream, completely losing herself in the moment as every muscle within her body clenches and releases in unison. She lifts up and slams back down a few times, riding through the climax with a wide smile on her face. All the while, I don't let up for a second, continuing to lick her pussy throughout the entire erotic ride.

When the video game finally finishes she collapses back against the ground in a satisfied mess. She's not finished, however, and the next thing I know the arcade cabinet is pulling me up onto her body. Soon enough, I'm straddling her hard frame while Henry continues to take me from behind.

While the cabinet behind me slams deep, Jessica starts to rub my clit with her fingers. The two of them begin to work together with an incredible sense of harmony, their movements creating a feeling deep within the pit of my stomach that is so much more than the sum of its parts. Something is happening between the three of us that's hard to describe, and as I stay here sandwiched between the two arcade games, I find myself feeling completely at home.

This is exactly where I need to be.

I can tell that Henry is about to explode, his hammering reaching a fever pitch as his body begins to quake and tremble like Jessica's before it. Fortunately, I'm on a similar timeline.

Before Henry even has a chance to cum I'm erupting with a climax of my own. The two gorgeous machines carry me over the edge with feverish, erotic gusto, moaning along with me as I throw my head back and howl. I close my eyes tight and let the sensations overwhelm me, satisfied in a way that no high score could ever hope to provide.

The second I finish Henry pulls out of me, the handsome arcade cabinet clenching his teeth as hot white spunk erupts from the head of his shaft. The jizz splatters out across my rump, painting my ass with beautiful pearly splatters that never seem to end.

When Henry finally finishes he falls back, panting wildly as he struggles to catch his breath.

"That was amazing," shaking my head in amazement. "I've never been to an arcade like this."

"Come back any time," Jessica offers. "I think that's a new record for me."

I notice now that the points across her screen are flashing brilliantly, the luminous digital letters declaring a new high score. Henry features a similar readout.

I stand up and begin to pull back on my clothes, ready to head home.

"You're not gonna stick around?" Jessica questions.

"Not tonight," I reply. "I'll be back, but right now I feel like relaxing at my local spot with a tall glass of chocolate milk and one of the classics."

"Then we'll see you soon," Jessica accepts with a smile.

"What are you gonna play?" Henry asks, curiously.

"There's a Space Raptor machine downtown with my name on it," I reply with a grin.

.

THESE BOOTS ARE MADE FOR POUNDING, AND THAT'S JUST WHAT THEY'LL DO, ONE OF THESE DAYS THESE BOOTS ARE GONNA POUND ME IN THE BUTT

"You seem stressed," my friend Jeremy finally offers after staring at me for quite some time.

We're sitting across from one another at the chocolate milk shop, sipping from our tall, cold glasses of the delicious beverage as we take a break from the summer heat. Out here on the patio there's plenty of shade, and the situation would otherwise be quite relaxing if not for the fact that Jeremy's right. I *am* stressed.

"It's this work presentation," I finally reply, shaking my head from side to side. "It's all I can think about."

My friend shrugs. "You've got work presentations all the time," he reminds me. "You've got this."

He's usually correct in his assertion that I'll make it out of the boardroom just fine, but I'm struggling to find the same amount of confidence in myself right now. It's not that I've gotten worse at my job, but recently it seems like everyone around me has gotten that much *better* at what they do. I'm having a hard time keeping up.

"Damn," Jeremy continues. "Usually you snap out of it at this point. I'm sorry, Derek."

"I know, I know," I reply, shaking my head from side to side. "I'm just not quite sure about the angle I'm taking. Tingle Enterprises loves originality in their outside pitches, but more than that, they love confidence.

If I don't go in there and take over the room, I'm a goner."

"So go in there and take over the room," Jeremy counters.

Easier said than done, I think to myself.

"Be honest with me. Is your idea good?" my friend continues. "Like, really good? Worth being excited about?"

I don't think twice. "Yeah, it's amazing. I've proposed building a four-ply crab suit for the lake. There's been three-ply crab suits available before, but four has never been done. It's bold, it's fresh… we could make it work."

"Then where's your confidence hiding?" Jeremy questions. "If the idea is so good then what's the problem?"

I consider his words, really wracking my brain but coming up with nothing. "I don't know," I finally admit. "I really don't know."

Just then a pair of velociraptors trot by us holding chocolate milk glasses of their own. They're talking and laughing together, completely wrapped up in their conversation, but there's something about them that instantly draws me and Jeremy in. They exude a social electricity that cannot be denied.

"I need that kind of confidence," I offer.

Jeremy laughs. "Well, that's easy. It's those boots."

I glace down and notice that, in fact, one of the dinosaurs strolling past us is wearing a pair of gorgeous boots the likes of which I've never seen. They're impeccably crafted, right down to the very last detail. I find myself instantly drawn to them in an almost supernatural way.

Without thinking, I leap up from my chair and run over to the dinosaurs, who are quite a bit down the sidewalk at this point.

"Excuse me," I call out.

The scaly prehistoric creatures turn around to gaze at me curiously.

"I'm so sorry, but I have to ask," I continue. "Where did you get those boots? They're incredible."

The dinosaurs laugh as they exchange knowing glances.

"It's no problem," the raptor offers. "I get asked about these boots a lot."

"I can see why. They're incredible," I remark.

"Well, thank you. I wish I could help you get your hands on a pair, but they're very, very hard to find," the raptor explains sympathetically. "I think you might be out of luck, buckaroo."

The dinosaurs turn to go but I find myself crying out to stop them.

"Wait," I stammer. "I've got a presentation at work and... I just need these shoes. I'll buy them off of you for whatever you want."

"I don't think we're the same size," the prehistoric creature laughs. He takes a deep breath and then lets it out slowly, considering something. "Listen," he finally continues, leaning in close. "I think I know where you can find a pair. Do you know where Mustang Springs is?"

"Mustang Springs?" I question. "Out in the desert? Isn't that a place where people hike?"

The dinosaur nods. "My boots have been talking about their friends out there in Mustang Springs," he informs me, glancing down at the shoes upon his feet. "You could probably head out and find them if you looked hard enough."

"Thank you," I reply with a gracious nod. "Thank you so much."

The raptors leave and I stroll back to Jeremy, a fire in my belly.

"How'd it go, Derek?" my friend questions.

"Really good," I reply. "Do you know where Mustang Springs is?"

I pull up to the trailhead and park, dust still wafting up around my car as I open the door and step out into the sunlight. It's a hot day, hot enough that even the bravest hikers have decided to stay home for the afternoon.

I think I can manage, though, and I've brought enough water to stay safe. My skin is lathered up with sunscreen and I've purchased an actual paper map of the area just in case I lose service on my phone.

I'll admit, it *has* crossed my mind that this could be some kind of elaborate prank from the dinosaur, the scaly creatures hoping to throw me off track in my attempt to bite their style. When I look back, however, there was something truly genuine about our encounter. The raptor understood that I was a man in need of help, like he'd once been before finding these incredible boots.

Eventually, I begin my trek up the path, enjoying the warm breeze as the dirt crunches below my feet. The first part of this hike is the most difficult, all of the elevation gains pushed into the beginning segments before things flatten out across a vast plateau on top. It's fine, really, especially because for this first brief while I get to enjoy the shade of the canyon.

I pass a few fellow outdoor enthusiasts along the trail, waving to them as I go, but eventually the crowds begin to fade away. Soon enough, any other sign of sentient life falls away.

The longer I go, however, the more skeptical I grow about the idea I could ever reach the bottom of this mystery. This is a vast area of wilderness, and there's very little information for me to work with. When I reach the top of the climb I can see quite far, but there's nothing out there that would suggest a pair of beauitfully crafted boots are anywhere to be found.

Eventually, the trail ends and I find myself with a very important choice. Most folks reach this point and turn around to head back, but I've got another option. Just because the dirt path ends, doesn't mean the wilderness does too.

I sit down on a log and begin to weigh my options, seriously considering the fact this might be nothing more than a wild goose chase. I pull out my canteen and unscrew the top, taking a long, satisfying gulp of the cool chocolate milk within. I replace to top and lean forward with my hands on my knees, resting for a moment.

Suddenly, I notice something on the ground before me. There are plenty of old tracks out here on this particular trail, but almost all of them belong to hiking shoes. These indentations are quite different, however, because they look much, much fancier.

"The boots," I sigh aloud, the words falling limply from my mouth.

I glance up and see that these tracks take off into the wilds, and I immediately begin to follow along behind them. My head down, I continue forward like this until eventually heading back down into another canyon, this one much more desolate and out of the way. Over here, there is no clear path, and certainly no hikers.

It's not long before the rocks and trees open up into a flat clearing. It's here that I see it, a small home tucked against the far canyon wall. It's quite nice, more like a modern luxury getaway then some rustic log cabin.

I'm finally here, yet I hesitate. I realize now that the thing keeping me from walking right up there and knocking on the front door is exactly the same thing I'm hoping to fix: confidence. I'm stuck in the middle, living in a perpetual state of limbo while the world passes me by.

I take a deep breath and let it out, using all of the focus I can muster as I force myself to step forward. It takes everything I can to push each foot in front of the next, continuing on until I end up standing before the front door.

I lift my hand up and knock.

"Coming!" someone calls out from deep inside, followed by a set of footsteps.

Suddenly, the door opens up to reveal the most beautiful left boot that I've ever seen in my life. She's so stunning that I let out a slight gasp, staggering back as I struggle to maintain my balance. It's the shoe I was looking for.

"Can I help you?" the sentient piece of footwear continues, pulling me back to reality.

"Oh, yeah," I stammer. "I'm sorry about that. My name is Derek and… I don't know how to say this… I saw a pair of you yesterday and I didn't know where to find you."

The boot smiles. "So you're looking to make a purchase?"

I nod.

"Come on in," the sentient footwear continues, stepping back and waving me inside.

I walk through the threshold and find myself greeted with the delicious scent of home cooking, mixed with some kind of rustic, piney flavor.

"Gary!" the boot calls out. "We've got a visitor who's looking for a new pair of shoes!"

The right boot comes around the corner to greet me with a firm handshake. He's just as gorgeous as his partner, strong and muscular with a playful smile and a sturdy jaw.

"Nice to meet you," Gary offers.

"I'm Derek," I reply.

"I'm Rebecca," the left boot informs me.

"Have a seat," Gary continues, motioning towards a chair in the living room while him and his partner drop onto the couch.

I do as I'm told, sitting down and trying my best to act natural. I realize now that my heart is slamming hard within my chest, my adrenaline racing despite this situation that otherwise seems quite relaxed. After all, these boots are incredibly warm and friendly, not a care in the world as they invite me into their home.

Maybe that's exactly the issue, I realize. Their cool confidence is almost intimidating in itself. This calmness makes me slowly realize just how tightly wound I really am.

"So, you want to buy us?" Gary begins. "What's the story?"

"Well," I reply. "I've got this presentation at work and it's just... very intimidating. I know my idea is a good one, but when I run through all the scenarios in my head it makes me realize that everyone else's ideas are just as likely to catch my bosses attention. In fact, I feel like they're pulling ahead while I'm slipping behind."

"Based on what?" the boot continues.

I consider this a moment, then shrug. "I don't know."

"You really *are* losing confidence in yourself," Rebecca chimes in. "You don't have any reason to, but I can tell that you're overflowing with anxiety."

I nod. "Yep."

We sit in silence for a moment before Gary clears his throat. "Well, it's a shame that I have to tell you this, but we're not for sale."

His words pierce through me like an icicle to the heart. I try my best not to react, but the expression on my face says it all. I was really counting on this pair to help me through my upcoming meeting, and without them I don't know what I'm going to do.

Maybe I'll just call in sick that day and skip the whole thing.

"Yeah," I finally offer, defeated. "I shouldn't have assumed. I'll just be going now."

I start to climb out of my chair but Rebecca raises her hand to stop me. I drop back down, confused.

"That doesn't mean we're not interested in helping you," the beautiful boot offers.

"Wait, really?" I question.

"Really," she continues. "After all, you came all the way out here to find us, so it's not like you don't have *any* confidence. You just need to learn how to harness it."

"Exactly," Gary replies. "You've just gotta learn to relax."

"And you can help me?" I question.

The boots exchange glances.

"Maybe," Gary offers. "There's a few exercises we could try."

Tension suddenly floods into the room between the three of us. It weighs heavy in the air, eventually making the feeling undeniable. Could this erotic spark that bubbles up inside me actually be mutual? It seems too crazy to even consider, but as I gaze across the room at the playful smiles of Gary and Rebecca, my doubts slowly begin to fade away.

"We don't get visitors very often," Rebecca finally continues, breaking the silence. "It'd be a shame for you to leave too soon."

The two boots stand up very slowly and begin to cross the room towards me. My breathing heavy, I try my best to stay calm, but I'm finding it harder and harder to maintain my composure.

The next thing I know, the living footwear are kneeling down on the floor before me, gazing up with aching, lustful eyes. The two of them reach up and unzip my pants, slowly tugging them down until my large, erect cock pops forth and bounces in the air before them. I watch as their eyes follow my rod, clearly excited by what they've stumbled across.

Moments later, Gary opens wide and takes my shaft between his lips.

I let out a long sigh of pleasure as I sink even deeper into my chair, relaxing my body as the handsome boot begins to orally service me. The shoe starts off slowly at first, taking his time with me as his partner watches closely. Rebecca is clearly enjoying the show, but I don't have time to focus on her just yet.

Instead, I tilt my head back and let a long, satisfied groan escape my lips, the sound pouring out of me as though it's an audible manifestation of my own overwhelming anxiety.

Gary begins to move faster and faster, pumping my cock between his lips until finally passing me on to Rebecca. The other boot wastes no time, getting to work immediately as Gary continues to cradle my balls.

Rebecca works me with just as much skill as her partner, sucking me offer with slow, graceful pumps. Eventually, she pulls me out and drags her tongue across my shaft from the base to the tip, then kisses the head of my cock playfully. Next, the living boot opens wide and swallows my rod again, only this time she doesn't pull back.

Instead, the sentient footwear takes my shaft farther and farther down within her, all the way to her sole as I fill the boot completely. Somehow she manages to relax her gag reflex, allowing my rod to slip down until I'm completely consumed in a stunning deep throat maneuver.

I place my hands against the back of the living boot's head, holding her for a moment until finally Rebecca pulls back with a loud gasp, spit dangling between her lips and the head of my shaft in a long, semi-translucent strand.

This is a lot of fun, and I suddenly find myself charged up with a potent energy that wasn't there before. It's not just the arousal that's propelling me, it's a confidence and an attitude that has bubbled up to the forefront of my personality. I feel like taking things into my own hands, to make this encounter play out in a way that's both fulfilling and fun.

"Now it's your turn," I offer.

I'm suddenly sliding down onto the floor and pushing Rebecca back. The boot moves along with me, sprawling out on the ground and opening her legs so that I can dive in. I quickly get to work, licking her clit with slow, steady movements while her partner looks on in awe.

It's not long before the other boot decides to join in, and the next thing I know he's right there on the ground next to me, lapping away at Rebecca's pussy. Me and the handsome boot trade positions back and forth, taking charge for a moment and then pulling back. Sometimes the two of us just start making out for a bit, using our hands to stimulate Rebecca before returning to the fray.

Clearly, the beautiful boot above likes this, because soon enough her body begins to tremble and quake. I slip two fingers deep within her but keep the pace with my tongue, not letting up for a second. I can feel the sentient boot's stomach clenching tight and then releasing in a series of spastic movements, pushing closer and closer to an orgasmic erupting until, finally, she explodes with a wild shriek. The boot cries out as her body trembles and quakes, completely losing herself in the moment.

"Oh fuck! I'm cumming so hard! That feels so fucking good!" she screams.

The orgasm seems to last forever, but when she finally finishes I continue to push this encounter onward. There's something that I'm craving, and I'm hoping these two can treat me to an adventure.

I move to the side slightly and I pull off the rest of my clothes, then climb up onto my hands and knees. I'm completely nude now, and I pop my bare ass out towards Gary as he stands behind me.

I turn and glance back over my shoulder at him coyly. "I want you to fuck me!" I demand.

The handsome boot doesn't need to be told twice, climbing down into position behind and aligning his enormous rod with my tightly puckered backdoor. I can feel him teasing me for a moment, gentling moving the head of his shaft across my puckered anal seal. Eventually, the living footwear has mercy and plunges deep down within my butthole.

I let out a startled yelp as the sentient boot enters me, not entirely prepared for Gary's enormous size. Although I'd just finished taking him in my mouth, the way his mammoth rod stretches out my ass is something else entirely.

Fortunately, Gary is happy to take his time with me. A patient lover, the sentient boot stays plunged deep within my butt and doesn't move, just rests there as he allows my rectum to adjust to his formidable size. Gradually, any discomfort begins to slip away, replaced instead by a pleasant, aching warmth that fills me to the brim.

Soon enough, Gary begins to thrust in and out of my body, fucking me in a series of deep, confident swoops. They start off slowly at first and then gradually gain speed, moving faster and faster until he's pounding away at my butt with a steady rhythm.

Meanwhile, Rebecca has taken it upon herself to climb down in front of my body. She scoots back until she's in the doggystyle position right below me, then pops her ass back in a similar fashion to my own.

"Fuck me," she demands, making her request in a simple and direct manner.

I reach down and grab ahold of my cock, then slip it within the boot. She groans loudly, biting her lip and then falling into a rhythm with me and Gary. The next thing I know, all three of us are hammering into each other like this, an undulating accordion of sex.

The sensation is incredible, and although I'd like to hold off on cumming as long as I possibly can, Gary is on another timeline. Suddenly, the handsome shoe pushes into me and holds tight, erupting with a hot load of jizz. His cum spills forth in several bursts, filling up my asshole until it spills out from my tightly packed rim.

"Oh, fuck yeah," I sigh as the boot pulls away, his seed spilling out of me and running down the back of my legs.

"Now it's my turn," Rebecca offers.

The next thing I know, the beautiful boot reaches back and pulls my rod out of her. She stands up and walks into the other room mysteriously.

I glance back at Gary, who just smiles with knowing excitement.

Soon enough, Rebecca returns with a brand new tool attached to her lower abdomen, and enormous strap-on cock jutting out proudly towards me.

"What do you think?" the living boot questions.

"I think I need that inside my ass right now," I demand, ravenous for this new synthetic dick.

Rebecca strolls around behind me and then crouches down. I can feel her aligning her rod with my blown out, cum filled asshole, but unlike Gary she doesn't hesitate or tease me. Instead, she swiftly thrusts deep into my rump, causing me to cry out and then brace myself on the floor below.

The sentient boot immediately falls into a rhythm, hammering away at my ass with everything she's got. The sensation is incredible, and Rebecca clearly knows what she's doing with that thing. The beautiful boot is hitting me in just the right way, every slam causing my prostate to tremble with excitement.

I could easily cum from this alone, but in the pursuit of pleasure I reach down between my legs and grab ahold of my hanging dick. I quickly get to work pumping my hand along my shaft in time with the slams up my backside, the two sources of pleasure swirling together and creating a powerful cocktail of ecstasy.

"Oh fuck, just like that. Oh fuck, just like that," I begin to stammer, repeating the words over and over again as my eyes roll back into my head. With every round my voice grows louder until, eventually, I'm screaming out at the top of my lungs. "Oh fuck, just like that!"

Suddenly, the climax strikes me hard. I scream out as my body spasms, hot white spunk erupting from the head of my shaft and splattering across the floor below. It continues to surge forth in a bountiful cascade, painting everything under me until I finally finish and fall to the side in a fucked silly daze.

"Oh my god, that was so fucking good," I groan.

The three of us sit here for a moment as we collect our senses.

"How do you feel?" Rebecca finally questions.

"I feel…" I begin, then take a moment to really consider her question. I take inventory of myself, trying my best to remain objective and truly analyze the situation at hand. "I feel confident." I offer.

The boot smiles. "Maybe you didn't actually need a new pair of boots," she suggests. "Maybe you just needed to believe in yourself."

"And a good fucking," Gary chimes in.

The three of us laugh. The dynamic in the room has definitely changed, and I notice it now. Before, I'd felt like an intruder here, not by coming to their home but simply by existing and taking up space. Now, it feels like all three of us are equal peers.

Eventually, I stand up and begin to pull on my clothes, preparing to leave.

The boots watch me, their eyes lingering across my body with a pleasant reverence.

"Thank you so much," I offer when it's finally time for me to leave. "You've really helped me out."

I turn to head out the door when suddenly Gary calls out to me from behind, stopping me in my tracks.

"Wait!" the boot yells.

"Yeah?" I reply, curiously.

"We might not be for sale, but you could always borrow us if you really wanted," he proposes.

"Really?" I question. "You'd want to come to the meeting?"

"For you? Sure," the handsome boot continues. "We're *made* for walking, might as well get some walking done."

"It's been a while since we've had a day in the city," Rebecca adds with a nod. "Sounds like fun. Especially with a new friend."

BISEXUAL MOTHMAN MAILMAN MAKES A SPECIAL DELIVERY

When you've been in a relationship for as long as we have, there are plenty of hurtles to face. Things always change of the course of a marriage, and that's just fine. In fact, they *should* change.

No one knows exactly why we've been placed here on this planet and given a chance to putter around, but evolving and growing seems to be a big part of it. Why wouldn't you want that for your partner? Or your relationship as a whole?

Fortunately, Ivy and I love each other from the bottom of our hearts in a way that not only supports change, it thrives on it. The two of us are always looking for adventure, and this desire for all things novel and new keeps us satisfied.

Typically, this personality trait manifests itself in a variety of trips around the world. Of course, we need to strike a balance between work and play, planning our vacation days accordingly, but you can bet that Ivy and me will be out of town as much as possible, taking in all the sights and sounds of some far off land.

Lately, however, work has been especially crazy for the both of us. Ivy's production company has taken on several new clients, each and every one of them sporting their own unique demands that can barely be satisfied. Meanwhile, as a professional writer, I've been working non-stop to get my new novel finished, and while this is typically something that I can do on the road, the deadline for this book is looming larger than ever. I need to buckle down and focus, which means the worldwide adventures will have to wait.

Now Ivy and I are posted up in either corner of our home, laptops open and screens crammed full of various tasks we've gotta accomplish before even *thinking* about taking a break. It's nice that my wife can work from home, too, so despite this incredible pressure to take care of business, we still have plenty of time to see each other.

"Can you get that?" my wife calls out, her voice echoing through my house and breaking my concentration. I'm abruptly pulled out of a passage I was deeply focused on.

I blink a few times, somehow hoping this tiny movement might center my brain. I turn away from my computer, calling back over my shoulder towards Ivy's end of the house. "Get what?"

"You didn't hear that?" my wife shouts in return.

"Hear what?" I continue, utterly confused.

Suddenly, the familiar ring of our doorbell echoes through our home. I must have been so deep into my writing that I'd missed it the first time.

Funny enough, as difficult as Ivy's work is, she's clearly less focused at the moment and in a much better position to grab the front door. Regardless, I'm happy to take care of it.

"Got it!" I call out, then stand up from my desk and walk through the living room towards the entryway. I catch a glimpse of my wife through the open door of her office as I go, giving her a playful wink.

I arrive at the front door and pull it open with a smile. "Hi there," I offer.

Standing before me is a mailman that I don't recognize. We've had Noah delivering packages for the six years that we've lived in this home, but it appears something has happened because the guy standing before me is certainly not Noah. Instead, I'm faced with a muscular mothman, the creature covered in greyish white hair and sporting a large pair of wings folded against his back. His eyes are huge and glowing, placed lower than one might expect and giving the rare cryptid a distinct appearance, as though his head was actually positioned somewhere deep within his muscular chest.

"Package for Ivy Herrington," the handsome mothman informs me, holding out a small box. "Anyone can sign for it, I just need a signature."

"Oh, thank you," I stammer. "Noah taking the day off?"

The mothman shakes his head, which consists of him turning his entire body from side to side. "Afraid not," the creature replies. "He's no longer with us."

"Oh, wow," I blurt. "I'm so sorry to hear that."

The mothman seems a little confused at first and then, moments later, his expression floods with understanding. "Oh no. He just quit."

The creature hands me a clipboard with a sheet of paper attached to the front of it. I sign it quickly and then hand it back to him.

"Thank you!" the mothman replies. "I'll be seeing you!"

The creature turns to leave but I call out to stop him in his tracks. "What's your name?" I question.

"Indrid!" the mothman replies. "Nice to meet you!"

"I'm Cooper," I inform him, reaching out and giving the furry, muscular creature a firm handshake.

The mothman smiles and then turns once again, heading off down the front walkway with a satchel full of packages slung over his shoulder. I can't help but let my eyes linger as he goes, taking in the creature's incredibly muscular physique. He's dressed quite conservatively, in a typical mail carrier's uniform, but the cut of his pants hang just right across the mothman's perfectly toned rump.

When he's finally out of sight I turn to head back inside, but jump in surprise when I see that my wife is standing in the foyer waiting for me.

"Oh!" I blurt, almost dropping the package. "I didn't see you there."

"You okay?" Ivy questions.

I nod, trying to pull myself back into reality. "Yeah, I just met the new mailman."

"Noah's gone?" my wife continues.

"Apparently," I reply, strolling over and handing her the package. "This is for you."

Ivy smiles and takes the box, then opens it immediately, tearing through the package and pulling out a brand new book. It's titled Bisexual Buckaroos: Seven Bi Group Encounters In The Tingleverse.

"That looks fun," I offer, taking in the gorgeous couple standing proudly on the cover between a dinosaur and a bigfoot.

My wife grins mischievously. "I thought we could read it together."

Initially, I'd planned on keeping my powerful attraction to the mothman mailman under wraps, just a fleeting moment in time and nothing more. It suddenly dawns on me, however, that Ivy might be just as interested in our handsome new mailman as I am.

We're an adventurous couple, after all, and if we don't have time to head out into the world and experience new things, maybe these new experiences can come to us.

"The mailman was… pretty cute," I finally inform her. "You would've liked him."

"Maybe *I'll* get the door next time," Ivy offers.

The two of us eventually get back to work in our separate ends of the house, but now I'm struggling to focus. I typically don't have much trouble diving back into projects, but the handsome mailman's cute butt keeps trotting through my head and distracting me. I keep typing out a few sentences at a time, then immediately lose my train of thought as a mothman rump strolls across my conscious mind, playfully swinging his hips from side to side.

Eventually, I give into my temptation. I open up an online shopping website and do a quick search for something, anything, that has same day delivery.

I settle on a brand new pen, then click to order.

The second my order is placed I feel a sense of calm and focus wash over me. I've done as much as I can to fulfill this strange little fantasy, and now it's time for me to let it go. Now, the only thing left to do is wait.

As the afternoon rolls onward, I actually manage to get some words down. I'm in the zone, rolling along confidently as my fingers dance across the keyboard before me. The handsome mothman is still lurking somewhere in the back of my mind, but right now he's certainly not the focus.

However, all of that changes when the doorbell rings.

I stand up from my chair, strolling out into the foyer to see that my wife is still working away, her headphones plugged in and her music blaring.

"Hey!" I call out. "Could you get the door?"

Ivy doesn't notice.

"Hey!" I continue.

Eventually, I'm forced to walk over and tap my wife on the shoulder, causing her to turn around and pull off her headphones.

"Can you get the door?" I question.

My wife just stares at me blankly. "Why don't you get it?"

This is a very good point, and suddenly I find myself completely unable to respond with a coherent answer. The next thing I know, Ivy and me are both laughing hysterically.

"I ordered something online," I finally explain once I get control of the spastic chuckles that are escaping my throat. "You can see the mailman now."

Ivy grins, shaking her head from side to side in an expression of good natured frustration and begrudging excitement. She takes a deep breath and stands up from her chair, then strolls out into the living room as she makes her way toward the front door. Meanwhile, I hang back and watch her go, sneaking glances from around the door frame of her office.

Ivy opens the door. "Hi there," she begins, then stops suddenly as the words catch in her throat.

"Is everything alright?" comes the familiar voice of our new mothman mailman.

"Oh, yeah," my wife stammers, struggling to collect herself. "I heard we had a new delivery person, but I guess I'm still a little surprised."

"That's alright. I'm Indrid," he continues. "It's nice to meet you."

"Ivy," my wife counters, introducing herself.

The mothman mailman hands Ivy my package. "Here you go," he offers. "Have a good day, ma'am."

Indrid strolls away and my wife slowly closes the door behind him. Her jaw is hanging open and her eyes are wide as she walks back to me. She mouths the words, "oh my god," as she approaches, then hands me the package before wrapping her arms around me.

"Right?" I offer.

"You weren't kidding," Ivy continues, kissing me deeply on the lips.

My heart is slamming hard within my chest now for reasons that I can't quite explain. That craving for adventure I've been longing for has finally been satiated in some small way, and now my body is desperate for more. I can tell that Ivy is on exactly the same page, and as we pull away from one another our eyes lock in a knowing gaze.

"Should we… order more packages?" my wife questions mischievously.

The mere suggestion sends a bolt of arousal through my body, but I find myself hesitating. As fun as this is, I certainly don't want to be a nuisance to our new mail carrier. I understand that he's just doing his job, and will be delivering mail all day regardless of whose house it's going to, but I still feel a little strange about ogling someone who doesn't want to be ogled.

"I don't know," I finally reply. "I don't wanna bother him if it's just for kicks."

"It might not be," Ivy offers.

I furrow my brow, not quite sure what she's getting at. "What do you mean?" I question.

"He winked at me," my wife continues.

Another bolt of arousal shoots through me, this one even more potent than the first. I can feel my frame starting to tremble slightly, quaking with a sense of anxious arousal.

"Really?" I question, this revelation seeming a little too good to be true.

"He sure did," Ivy offers. "Let's just order a few more packages and see what happens."

Over the next few days, my wife and I make far more online purchases than we probably should. We make sure to space them out so they arrive slowly, coming throughout the afternoons and allowing us a steady stream of interaction with Indrid the mailman.

It's not long before we strike up a casual report with this handsome mothman, learning all about his life and growing ever more attracted by his laidback confidence. We learn a lot over the course of those few days, like the fact that mothmen are technically a species of bigfoot, and that Indrid could make his rounds much faster with the use of his wings, but he's required to drive the mail truck for advertising purposes.

It also becomes glaringly apparent that Indrid's attraction is not just towards my wife, but me as well.

Soon enough, all three of us are openly flirting whenever he arrives, growing more and more blatant with our advances as the erotic tension builds.

Finally, Ivy and I hatch a plan.

The doorbell rings and my wife and I exchange glances.

"Are you sure you wanna do this?" I question.

Ivy nods, taking my hand in hers and then giving me a quick kiss.

We stroll over to the front door and open it up, smiling wide as we're greeted by Indrid's familiar face.

"Two packages for my favorite folks!" the mothman announces, handing us our respective boxes. "How you doing this afternoon?"

"Pretty good," I reply. "Excited to get these open."

"Oh yeah?" the mothman continues. "Something fun?"

My wife grins mischievously, then reaches out and runs her hand down Indrid's muscular chest, a move that clearly tips our usual flirtatious conversation into something much, much more. This is the moment that everything could change, Indrid's opportunity to pull away and shut the whole scenario down, or decide to push even deeper into uncharted waters.

"You wanna come in and open up these packages with us?" Ivy questions.

I'm utterly frozen in place, waiting with baited breath to see what our cryptid mailman's reaction will be.

The mothman smiles, understanding exactly what's going on here. "It's my duty as a mailman to make sure all packages get where they're going in working order," he replies slyly.

We step back and open the door even wider so that Ingrid can step inside. The mailman comes in and takes a look around, admiring this home from a viewpoint he's never had before.

"Which one should we open first?" my wife continues.

The mothman smiles and then turns his attention to me. "How about yours?"

I nod, then begin to slowly, but confidently, tear open my brown box. Moments later, I extract an object from within: a rubber cock ring.

"Very nice," Indrid offers. "Let's make sure it wasn't damaged in transit."

The handsome cryptid reaches down and begins to unbutton my jeans, eventually tugging them down and allowing my swollen cock to spring forth in all of its glory. Indrid gasps slightly when he first lays eyes on my enormous rod, but quickly centers himself.

The mothman mailman takes my cock ring and then drops down to his knees before me, gazing up playfully as he takes my dick in one hand. With the other hand he positions my new cock ring and then starts to push it down across my shaft.

Unfortunately, this doesn't seem to work. A little more lubrication is required.

"Let's get you wet," Indrid offers.

The next thing I know, the handsome mothman is opening his mouth wide and taking my rock hard dick between his lips, slowly pumping his face up and down across the length of my shaft. I lean my head back and let out a long, satisfied groan, my eyes shut tight as I bask in this incredible moment of pleasure.

Soon enough, I sense another presence joining the handsome mothman below. I glance down to see my beautiful wife, also on her knees, taking turns with some oral maneuvers of her own. My two lovers begin to pass my shaft back and forth, sometimes dragging their tongues across my length and other times sucking me off with frantic enthusiasm. My wife reaches up and cradles my balls as she works me, a technique that she knows I enjoy.

Soon enough, the whole encounter evolves into some kind of spirited competition between Indrid and Ivy, showing off their blowjob skills in a playful sexual contest.

It's not long before Ivy opens her mouth wide and takes my cock between her lips, pushing her face farther down onto my shaft. Deeper and deeper she slides, swallowing my entire cock within her gullet and somehow relaxing her gag reflex enough to provide me safe passage. The next thing I know, my wife's face is pressed up hard against my toned abs, my member fully consumed in a stunning deep throat.

I place my hands on the back of my wife's head, holding her here for a good while until Ivy is finally forced to pull back in a sputtering gasp, spit dangling in a long, translucent strand between her lips and the head of my shaft.

"There we go," Ingrid offers cheerfully, grabbing my dick once more and placing my new cock ring over the end. He slides the rubber circle all the way down to the base and then moves back a bit, admiring his handiwork.

"Think it fits?" I question playfully.

"Looks perfect," the mothman mailman observes. "Now let's take it for a test drive in my ass."

The handsome cryptid turns around and falls forward, popping his butt out toward me and wiggling his furry rump from side to side. He begins to slip out of his uniform, pulling the fabric away from his body slowly and revealing a breathtakingly chiseled form. Soon enough, Indrid is completely naked.

He reaches back and gives his rear end a playful slap, gripping his butt tightly with one hand and then spreading himself open so that I can get a good look.

"What are you waiting for?" Indrid coos. "Come fuck this tight mothman ass."

"You heard him," my wife chimes in enthusiastically.

I do as I'm told, climbing down into position behind the handsome mailman and aligning my swollen dick with his tightly puckered backdoor. I tease the rim of his butthole for a minute and then finally push forward in a deep, powerful swoop, watching with rapt amazing as the creature leans back and lets out a long, satisfied moan.

The mothman braces himself against me so that my cock can plunge even deeper within his stretched out asshole. He takes me fully as the two of us begin to rock together, enjoying the pleasant sensations as they spill forth across our bodies. We start slowly at first, then gradually speed up into a steady rhythm.

"Keep fucking me, keep fucking me," the mothman groans, repeating the words over and over in a frantic mantra. He starts off quiet and then builds into a wild scream, crying out over and over again while I hammer him from behind. "Keep fucking me! Keep fucking me!"

Suddenly, the familiar voice of my beautiful wife cuts through the commotion. "Should we see if my package is in working order, too?" she questions.

The mothman and I look up to see Ivy standing proudly before us, an enormous strap-on cock projecting out from her hips.

Indrid and I nod vigorously, watching with excitement as my wife strolls around behind me. She spits on her hand, lubing up her new toy, then positions herself at the rear. The three of us are now hunched over in a long row of pleasure, stacked like pleasure seeking dominoes just ready to fall over the edge of orgasm.

Ivy wastes no time, thrusting forward and impaling me across her strap-on rod. I let out a startled yelp as she enters me, not entirely prepared for her incredible size but accepting it all the same.

My wife takes her time with me, holding still at first as she allows my body to adjust to her gigantic shaft. Eventually, the two of us start to move, any discomfort slipping away as it's replaced by a potent warmth and fullness.

Soon enough, all three of us are bucking against one another, our bodies slamming in a expertly performed polyrhythmic dance. We begin to loudly moan in a chorus of ecstasy, our voices swirling like a sonic cocktail as the sensations build within.

My position in the middle is almost too overwhelming, but I somehow manage to stay connected to this moment. The pleasure that floods through me is just as much about my cock in Indrid's ass as it is the strap-on that's impaled mine.

"I'm so close!" I cry out.

"Not yet," my wife coos in my ear. "I want *you* to fuck *me* now."

Ivy pulls out and, moments later, I remove myself from the handsome mothman.

The three of us turn around in unison so that our established connections have been reversed. Instead of my dick fucking Indrid, the muscular cryptid is now preparing himself to plow away at me. My wife, on the other hand, have flipped around and is laying out on her back with her legs spread confidently. She looks absolutely incredible, offering me a mischievous wink as I climb down into position before her.

Ivy takes a moment to remove her strap-on so that I'll have easier access, then wraps her arms around me, pulling me close. I slip deep within my wife's pussy, sighing loudly as she accepts me into her warmth.

"Are you having fun?" Ivy whispers in my ear.

I nod enthusiastically. "Fuck yes."

Suddenly, the mothman enters me from behind and causes my breath to catch in my throat. I'd thought my wife's strap-on was big, but this is another level entirely. Indrid's cock is a force to be reckoned with, and I'm lucky I've been significantly warmed up.

As I thrust into my beautiful wife, the mailman slams into me from behind with equal force, grinding his hips against me as his mammoth cock drives deep. Indrid knows exactly what he's doing, his rod hitting me in just the right spot as the sensations of prostate orgasm begin to blossom.

It's not long before all three of us are crying out once more, that same ol' erotic choir singing a brand new song.

"Oh fuck, I'm gonna cum!" I yell, the aching pleasure building up within as I tremble and shake.

"Me too!" the mothman shrieks.

"Me three!" my wife adds, her eyes rolling back into her head.

Indrid goes first, hammering away at my butthole and then pushing deep and holding tight. I can feel his spunk spilling out in load after hot load, filling me up to the brim and then eventually spilling out from the corners of my tightly packed asshole. His cum runs down the back of my legs in long pearly streaks.

The feeling of the mothman's payload is enough to send me over the edge of my own mighty orgasm. I throw my head back and let out a wild, guttural cry, pulling out of Ivy's pussy and intending to blow my load all over the stomach of my wife. The second I do this, the mothman reaches around and grabs my dick in his furry hand, beating me off furiously as the orgasm hits me like a truck.

I buckle forward, almost collapsing entirely but somehow managing to stay upright as splatters of warm jizz erupt out from the head of my shaft. The jizz paints Ivy's skin with beautiful patterns as she reaches down and begins to frantically rub her clit.

The second I finish I dive down and begin to eat my wife out, lapping away at Ivy's pussy as her stomach begins to clench tight and then release over and over again.

"I wanna cum with a mothman cock in my ass," my wife suddenly coos, letting us know what she really wants.

I glance over at Indrid, who I expect to be tuckered out by now, but the handsome cryptid is already at full attention once more. The mothman springs into action, lying down next to my wife and helping her move as she climbs over the top of him.

Ivy reaches down and grabs Indrid's giant cock, then impales herself across his incredible girth in one swift and fearless movement. She doesn't move, just keeps the rod planted deep within her body as she pulls me back towards her pussy. The next thing I know, I'm flicking my tongue across Ivy's clit once again, pushing her closer and closer to the edge until she's tumbling over.

Seconds later my wife screams out and grips tightly onto the back of my head, pulling me against her as a powerful orgasm erupts through every nerve.

When the three of us finally finish we collapse into a pile right there in the middle of the living room, panting hard as we struggle to catch our breath.

"That was amazing," I finally offer.

"Agreed," the mothman replies, standing up and beginning to pull back on his uniform.

"Leaving so soon?" my wife coos.

Indrid nods. "I've still got a lot of packages on my list today," he informs us, "but you'll be seeing me around."

"I hope so," I chime in.

When the handsome cryptid finally finishes getting ready he strolls toward the front door, but stops before making his exit. Indrid turns back around to face us. "I'm looking forward to more special deliveries," he offers.

"Us too," I reply with a knowing grin.

BISEXUALLY BANGED BY THE ABSURD VOLUME OF CHUCK TINGLE'S LITERARY CATALOG

I stare at the blank screen before me, watching the cursor blink in a slowly, rhythmic pulse. It seems like I've been sitting here forever, waiting for inspiration to strike, yet it refuses to come. Has that much time really passed?

I glance over at a clock hanging on the wall of my living room, taking note of the time and feeling a flood of disappointment overwhelm me. I've been sitting here on my laptop doing nothing for a full hour now, just begging the hands of fate to reach down and push this story out of my brain and onto the page like a tube of toothpaste.

I know all of the beats, each and every moment meticulously planned out beforehand on the corkboard that hangs nearby. I've envisioned this opening scene a thousand different times and in a thousand different ways, and now is the moment to strike, to reach down and let my fingers dance freely across the keyboard.

This is supposed to be the easy part.

I let out a long sigh, finally breaking away from the computer and standing up from my desk. I stroll over to the corkboard and look it over. Despite my inability to get started, I'm certainly proud of what I've accomplished over here, the web of storylines and character arcs weaving together in perfect harmony with one another. It's really something to behold, and I have no doubt my novel will eventually reflect the wonder and amazement that I feel while looking this over.

I've just gotta start typing.

I turn to head back toward my computer when suddenly I stop in my tracks, then focus my attention squarely upon the corkboard once again. Maybe the reason I can't write is because the opening scene is better suited for a moment of rising action during the break into act three.

"That could work," I mumble under my breath, returning to the board and taking the first note card down.

My eyes dance back and forth across the various color coded rectangles, searching for an opening that makes sense and then finally settling on one near the end. Of course, this throws off the flow slightly, so I continue along, making a number of alterations that starts small and then slowly blossom into something much, much more.

By the time I step away from the corkboard, the original layout is completely unrecognizable. It's a frightening sight, but maybe it'll all be worth it once I start typing.

I reach out and take the first card in my hands, confidently reading it over to myself as I prepare to dive in.

Unfortunately, this new scene makes absolutely no sense as an opening.

"Oh shit," I blurt, suddenly thrown into a state of panic. I begin to frantically swap the cards around, struggling to get them back into the positions they started in, but gradually realizing I'm just wandering farther and farther off track.

In my organizational frenzy, I suddenly hit the board just a little too hard. The next thing I know, the entire thing is plummeting down, sliding off the wall and smashing onto the hardwood floor of my apartment with a loud clatter. The wooden frame cracks and the cards spill everywhere, scattering across the ground in an unsortable mess.

I freeze, tempted to scream out in agony but holding it together in a state of seething frustration.

I don't move to pick up the cards, leaving them exactly where they are. Instead, I simply walk toward the door of my apartment and head outside.

The second the sun and fresh air hit me I feel a wave of sweet relief. The house had started to suffocate me, and the pressure to create had simply grown too oppressive.

I stroll out to the sidewalk and make my way down the street, eventually arriving at the end of the block and then taking a sharp left. I continue a bit longer and soon enough I find myself standing on the front porch of my best friend, Renny.

I knock three times, waiting until the door opens then smiling with relief when I see my bestie standing before me.

"What's up?" Renny questions, immediately noting the frustration on my face.

"Wanna go on a walk?" I ask.

Renny nods, putting on her shoes then stepping outside and locking the door behind her. Soon enough, the two of us are strolling back down her front steps and making our way along the sidewalk.

"You seem a little wound up, Patrick," she offers.

"I am," I reply, nodding along as an admission of my utter failure. "It's the book."

"Oh yes, *the book,*" Renny repeats back to me, my answer making perfect sense. She's been following along since the beginning of my journey, and she knows how hard I've been working on this first novel. She also knows specifically what a difficult time I've had getting started.

"I don't know what to do," I continue, a surprisingly vulnerable tone slipping into my voice.

"Well, it's all mapped out," Renny offers. "Just start copying down what's on your note cards and then embellishing from there."

We stroll in silence for a moment as I hesitate to answer. Finally, I crack. "*Was,*" is all I say.

"What?" Renny counters, confused.

"It *was* all mapped out," I offer. "Now there are cards all over my floor."

My friend nods understandingly, patting me on the shoulder with loving reassurance. "I wish I was a writer so I could help you out, but I'm just about the least creative person you'll ever meet. I don't have much in the way of advice."

"It's fine, it's fine," I assure Renny.

The two of us stop on the corner, our walk coming to a brief moment of hesitation while we wait to cross and a large truck rumbles by. As we wait, I glance up at a billboard hanging nearby, the massive, colorful display announcing itself over the neighborhood corner store.

The old image must've been recently replaced, because I hadn't seen this new advertisement until now. The billboard is scattered with various depictions of book covers, the stories dancing across the background while one cover image in particular is featured front and center. Next to it is a smiling man in a Tae Kwon Do gi, a pink bag over his head and sunglasses covering his eyes. He's giving a thumbs up.

I read the billboard aloud, gazing at the bold words that stretch out across the bottom of this image. "New tingler, *Bisexually Banged By The Absurd Volume Of Chuck Tingle's Literary Catalog,* out now!"

The truck has long since passed, but Renny and I are still staring up at the billboard.

"Why don't you ask Chuck Tingle how he writes so many books?" my friend questions. "He's got like three hundred titles and four more seem to come out every week."

I consider this for a moment. Renny has already told me that she can't offer much advice about how to get started, but the suggestion of approaching a fellow author is actually a really good one.

"Do you think he'd reply if I sent him an email?" I question.

Renny shrugs. "Maybe. If you *really* want an answer you should just track him down in person."

I hadn't considered this was a possibility, but desperate times call for desperate measures. Chuck Tingle is notoriously strict about his privacy, and I doubt I'll actually be able to find him, but the journey alone might be enough to light a spark of creativity within. Whether I find Chuck or not, it's hard to imagine still having writer's block after putting in the effort.

"We're a long way from Billings," I finally reply. "That's where he's from, right?"

Renny nods. "It's possible. Some say he's actually a sentient artificial intelligence being held on a server farm in Nevada."

I raise one eyebrow. "Wait, really?"

"It's true," my friend continues, then stops herself, backing up a bit. "I mean, it's true people say that. I don't know if he really is."

"Well, what do *you* think?" I continue. "How am I supposed to find this guy?"

Renny turns back to the billboard, then points to the corner. At first I'm not entirely sure what I'm looking at, squinting my eyes to make out the tiny logo that's been emblazoned in white lettering.

"Paid for by The Sam Rand Company," I read aloud, then turn back to my friend. "Who is Sam Rand?"

"He runs Chuck's website and helps with the publishing side of things," Renny explains. "Rumor has it, he lives right here in the City of Devils. If you find Sam Rand, he can probably put you in touch with Chuck."

I pull out my phone and do a quick internet search for The Sam Rand Company, which brings me to a very simple and inconspicuous webpage. This page features the same logo that appears on the billboard before me, as well as a phone number with a City of Devils area code.

"Call it," Renny chides.

I dial the number and hold my phone to my ear as it rings once, twice, three times.

Finally, someone picks up.

"The Sam Rand Company," comes a woman's voice on the other end of the line.

"Oh, hi," I stammer, thrilled to make this call and now suddenly finding myself at a loss for words. I struggle to collect myself, desperately attempting to pull it together at this pivotal moment of my search. "My name is Patrick and I'm calling to see if I can set up a meeting with Sam Rand."

"Are you a character?" the voice on the other end of the line continues.

"You mean like… am I funny?" I ask, not quite understanding what she means.

"No. Are you a fictional character in one of Chuck's books?" the woman continues.

"Oh," I blurt, still not entirely sure if she's being serious but answering anyway. "No."

"I'm sorry, I can't help you," the voice replies.

I start to respond but before the words can even escape my lips the line goes dead.

I pull my phone away from my head and look down at it, as expression of utter confusion plastered across my face.

"What happened?" Renny asks.

"I'm not sure," I offer. "She asked if I was a character in a book. I said no and then she hung up."

"Then call back and say yes," my friend encourages.

"You mean lie?" I continues. "This is absurd."

"What other option do you have?" Renny astutely points out.

I let out a long sigh and dial the number again. This time it rings only once before they pick up, as though they were expecting a call back.

"The Sam Rand Company," comes the same voice on the other end of the line.

"Hi, this is a character in a book," I blurt.

There's a moment of silence, then finally the voice continues. "Alright, and which book are you currently in?"

My eyes go wide, definitely not expecting a follow up question like this. Frantically, I glance around for inspiration, my eyes immediately finding the enormous billboard that fueled this phone call in the first place. I cling onto the specific book they're advertising.

"Oh, I'm a character in *Bisexually Banged By The Absurd Volume Of Chuck Tingle's Literary Catalog*," I offer.

There's another brief silence on the other end of the line. This time I can hear someone typing swiftly across a computer keyboard, the sound faintly dancing across my ears.

"And how can we help you?" the voice asks.

"I'd like to speak with Sam Rand," I reply.

"Alright, we can send a car for you right away," the voice offers.

I open my mouth to respond but before I get a chance a shiny black limousine pulls up to the curb before Renny and me. It stops abruptly, and moments later the door pops open and slowly drifts wide to allow me entry.

"I think it's already here," I finally reply.

"Good, we'll see you soon," the voice concludes before hanging up.

I turn to Renny. "You coming with?" I question.

My friend hesitates. "I mean, I will if you want me to, but it seems like this mission is personal."

She's right.

We hug and then I climb into the limo. The next thing I know, I'm headed off through the streets of the City of Devils. I gaze though my window at the passing streets, struggling to determine where we're headed. I can't even see the driver up front, the two of us separated by a dark partition.

We don't cruise for long. Eventually, the limousine pulls over at a tall office building that I'd never noticed before.

The second I close the limo door it pulls away, leaving me standing here as I stare up at the enormous structure. Without much else to do, I approach the building, immediately stopped by a floating, sentient book in uniform. His title is *Slammed In The Butt By The Prehistoric Megalodon Shark Amid Accusations Of Jumping Over Him.*

"Name?" the book questions, stopping me in my tracks.

"I'm Patrick," I offer. "I'm here to see Sam Rand."

The sentient book chuckles to himself as I say this, glancing down at a clipboard and then waving me through.

I continue onward, stepping through a large turnstile and swiftly finding myself in a huge, luxurious lobby. Another book is floating behind a counter to my left, while directly forward is a large elevator bay.

A third book approaches quickly, extending her hand. "Hi there, I'm *Sentient Lesbian Jet Ski Gets Me Off* the living collection of words offers. "We spoke on the phone."

"Oh hey," I blurt, giving her a firm shake. "It's nice to meet you."

"Likewise," the book replies. "It's always great to see characters taking proactive steps to drive the plot forward."

I'm not entirely sure what she means by this, but I go with it, nodding along.

"So you're here to meet with Sam Rand?" she continues.

I nod.

"May I ask what this meeting is in regard to?" *Sentient Lesbian Jet Ski Gets Me Off* questions.

I consider another lie, but at this point I'm not interested in digging myself into a hole that I can't get out of. I hate making stuff up and stretching the truth like this anyway, so instead I opt to drop the act and explain what's really going on.

"I wanna meet Sam," I explain, "but the person I'm really hoping to talk to is Chuck Tingle. I was hoping that Sam Rand could help me get in touch with him."

"You could always email Chuck," the living book offers.

"I figured I'd make an adventure out of it," I admit. "Seemed more likely I'd get a response this way."

Sentient Lesbian Jet Ski Gets Me Off laughs. "You're the protagonist, so you'd get a response either way, but like I said, it's great to see someone driving the plot forward like this."

We stand here for a moment in awkward silence.

"So... can I meet Sam?" I question.

"Oh yes, sorry about that," the sentient book replies. "Actually, you're in luck. You can meet Chuck, too."

"Wait, really?" I blurt. "He's here?"

The living collection of words nods. "You can ask him anything you want."

Sentient Lesbian Jet Ski Gets Me Off turns and begins to lead me toward the bay of elevators, nodding at the book behind the desk as we go. Now that I get a closer look, I can see that he's none other than Chuck's bestselling tingler, *Bigfoot Pirates Haunt My Balls.*

"Do all the books work here?" I question as my hostess reaches an elevator and presses the call button.

"Yes," she replies with a nod, "Including several that haven't even been written yet."

Sentient Lesbian Jet Ski Gets Me Off motions toward a beautiful book who enters the lobby behind us and starts chatting it up with the collection of words behind the counter.

"See her?" *Sentient Lesbian Jet Ski Gets Me Off* questions. "That's *Mercury Is In Retrograde And She Eats My Ass,* she won't be out for a while. Right now she's just a little kernel of an idea bouncing around in Chuck Tingle's mind."

"Whoa," is all I can think to say, taking it all in.

The elevator doors open before us and we step inside. *Sentient Lesbian Jet Ski Gets Me Off* presses the button for the top floor, which happens to be floor sixty-nine.

"The sex number," the book informs me.

"Nice," I reply, nodding my head.

Soon the elevator is traveling upward, the anxiety within me building as I realize how close I'm getting to a breathtakingly important moment in my journey as an artist. Of course, Sam and Chuck might have nothing to say by way of advice, but I doubt it. Chuck Tingle has been way too successful to not have *some* kind of wisdom to impart on me, especially after putting in the effort to track him down.

Our lift finally stops and the doors slide open, revealing a long hallway. *Sentient Lesbian Jet Ski Gets Me Off* and I begin to walk down it, making our way toward a large set of wooden double doors at the end.

The hall is lined with several framed portraits, and although I don't know much about Chuck Tingle's life, I can still pick out a few familiar faces that he often talks about.

One of the photos in particular catches my eye. It's of a woman in a long dress, hovering in a dark room with several black tentacles erupting from her back. Her head is hung low but you can still see a strange darkness in her eyes as water drips from her mouth. Her skin is pale and bluish in hue, as though she's been trapped under cold water for far too long.

"Is that Chuck's wife, Sweet Barbara?" I question.

Sentient Lesbian Jet Ski Gets Me Off nods. "It sure is. Over there is Son Jon, and the next one is Klowy."

I continue down the hallway, observing Chuck's inner circle. I see a man covered in stubble wearing a trucker's hat that has "love to stab" written across the front of it in bold lettering, the word love represented by a large red heart.

I see a man in a black and white photo with a long beard and a fishman's hat. He's standing on the deck of an old boat while the endless ocean stretches out behind him.

I even notice that one of the portraits is turned around, hanging on the wall but facing the other way.

"Who is that of?" I question.

"Ted Cobbler," *Sentient Lesbian Jet Ski Gets Me Off* informs me.

Eventually, we reach the double doors. I realize suddenly that I'm trembling slightly, the anxiety within me blossoming to a peak and now manifesting itself as a physical force.

I take a deep breath and then let it out, hesitating before pushing onward.

"It's okay," *Sentient Lesbian Jet Ski Gets Me Off* offers, putting her hand on my shoulder. "Ninety-nine percent of tinglers have a happy ending."

I'm not entirely sure what she means by this, but her tone and expression alone are enough to put me slightly at ease.

Finally, I push through the doors.

Before me is a boardroom with a large, oval table in the middle. Beyond this is a glorious view of the City of Devils, stretching out for what seems like forever and then finally arriving at the looming Tinglewood Hills.

Chuck Tingle and Sam Rand, however, are nowhere to be found.

Instead, each of the six boardroom seats is taken up by one of Chuck Tingle's books. Gazing from one chair to the next, I see *Bisexual Polyhedral*

Role-Playing Dice Orgy, Sentient Bisexual Ketchup And Mustard Get Me Off, The Sun And The Moon Bang Me Bisexually, Bisexual Arcade Machines Work My Slot, Bisexual Mothman Mailman Makes A Special Delivery In Our Butts, and *We Are Loving Bisexuals And They Are Living Bicycles.*

I narrow my eyes. "Where's Chuck and Sam?"

I turn my attention back to *Sentient Lesbian Jet Ski Gets Me Off,* who is now backing out of the room and closing the doors behind her. "I think you all have some talking to do," she offers awkwardly.

Bisexual Arcade Machines Work My Slot stands up from her chair and approaches. "There is no Sam Rand," she informs me.

"What?" I blurt.

"There is no Chuck Tingle either," she continues.

"Then who's writing you?" I question.

The whole boardroom exchanges glances with one another, clearly in on an important piece of information that I'm not yet privy to.

"We wrote ourselves," *Bisexual Arcade Machines Work My Slot* finally informs me. "We are a self-sustaining collective organism, growing larger and larger every day."

"But…" I stammer, shaking my head in amazement. "That doesn't make any sense. If you wrote yourselves then who authored the first book?"

"We don't claim to understand the spark of creation for sentient books any more than we do for humans," *Bisexual Arcade Machines Work My Slot* replies.

A sense of disappointment immediately floods over me, suddenly realizing that I'll probably never find the advice I'm looking for.

"That's actually why I'm here," I admit. "I need help understanding that spark for myself. I thought Sam and Chuck could help with a little advice on how to write a book of my own, but now I realize *they* don't even know."

"Well, on this timeline *they* don't exist," the book reminds me, "but I can offer you a bit of advice if you'd like."

I perk up a bit. "Really? What is it?"

"If you're having trouble with your story, maybe that's because you're not yet aware of your place in it," *Bisexual Arcade Machines Work My Slot* explains. "We're all the hero of our own story, sometimes more literally than we're even aware."

"How am I supposed to tell which story is my own?" I question.

"The one that proves love is real," *Bisexual Arcade Machines Work My Slot* replies. "Does the story you're trying to write prove love is real?"

"I don't know," I admit. "I was actually just trying to make something publishers would wanna buy."

The whole boardroom erupts in a fit of laughter, shaking their heads and rolling their eyes.

Bisexual Arcade Machines Work My Slot reaches out and pats me on the shoulder. "That's not your story then," she explains. "Your story is a bisexual message of sexy, meta fun wrapped up in the skin of an erotic short, but actually delivering this message…"

The sentient book turns and motions toward *The Sun And The Moon Bang Me Bisexually,* who pulls a string and unfurls a large banner hangin across the ceiling. Confetti and streamers fall as the boardroom cheers.

"Create with love and your art will find a way," I read aloud.

"That's right," *Bisexual Arcade Machines Work My Slot* confirms. "It might not always equate to huge sales, but it *will* equate to huge returns in other ways."

"And sometimes huge sales, too!" *Sentient Bisexual Ketchup And Mustard Get Me Off* calls out from her chair. "Just look at Chuck Tingle!"

"I thought Chuck wasn't real," I question.

"Depends on the timeline," *Bisexual Arcade Machines Work My Slot* reminds me. "I mean, technically speaking we're not just books, we're actually a physical manifestation of the absurd volume of Chuck Tingle's literary catalog. Therefore, Chuck Tingle is probably out there somewhere."

"He's probably writing this as we speak!" *We Are Loving Bisexuals And They Are Living Bicycles* chimes in.

"So… how does my story end?" I question.

"Well, it *could* end right now if you wanted," *Bisexual Arcade Machines Work My Slot* informs me, "We've already hit our word count, after all."

"Or?" I continue, not quite satisfied with this answer.

"You tell me," the book continues. "You're the star."

I consider her words for a moment, taking them to heart and then making my decision. Like I was told earlier, everyone likes a protagonist with some forward momentum.

"Stand up," I finally command the room.

The collection of bisexual books does as they're told, three men and three women, all of them absolutely gorgeous.

"Let's get this meeting started," I continue. "Get over here."

The next thing I know, the books have me surrounded, kissing me passionately from every angle. I lose track of who is who as their hands caress and touch my body, tearing away my clothing and tossing it to the side as my cock swells.

One of the sentient books reaches down and wraps their hand around my dick, slowly beating me off as a startled gasp escapes my throat.

"Oh fuck," I moan, leaning my head back as shutting my eyes tight.

Suddenly, the sensation changes. I glance down to see that *Bisexual Polyhedral Role-Playing Dice Orgy* has my cock between his lips, pumping his head up and down my shaft with graceful enthusiasm. Meanwhile, *We Are Loving Bisexuals And They Are Living Bicycles* cradles my balls in her hands, helping us along.

Bisexual Polyhedral Role-Playing Dice Orgy pumps faster and faster until he finally pulls back with a frantic gasp, passing my rod on to another gorgeous living book.

This time, *The Sun And The Moon Bang Me Bisexually* takes the reins, opening his lips wide and then swallowing my cock once again. Instead of frantic pumps, *The Sun And The Moon Bang Me Bisexually* simply pushes his face farther and farther down across my shaft, somehow relaxing enough to allow me passage beyond his gag reflex. Soon enough, the book's face is pressed up hard against my abs, consuming me fully in a stunning deep throat.

He holds here for quite a while, the rest of the books watching in stunned amazement at this incredible deep throat maneuver. The physical manifestation of the absurd volume of Chuck Tingle's literary catalog erupts in an enthusiastic cheer when *The Sun And The Moon Bang Me Bisexually* finally pulls away, a long strand of saliva hanging between his lips and the head of my cock.

The next thing I know, *Sentient Bisexual Ketchup And Mustard Get Me Off* grabs me by the hand and pulls me toward her. She maneuvers us over to the boardroom table, sitting up on the edge and spreading her legs. The book opens her arms and wraps them around me, pulling me close and kissing me deeply on the mouth.

I can see now that the rest of the books have broken off into their own groups, various pairings making out with one another passionately. Some of them are embracing as couples, while others are working each other in groups of three or four.

I also notice there are way more sentient books here than there were earlier. I glance around to see an assortment of tinglers, some of them old classics while others haven't even been written yet.

To my right, *Space Raptor Butt Invasion* and *Fake News, Real Boners* slam away in the heat of passion. Meanwhile, *Pounded In The Butt By My Own Butt*, *Pounded In The Butt By My Book "Pounded In The Butt By My Own Butt"*, *Pounded In The Butt By My Book "Pounded In The Butt By My Book 'Pounded In The Butt By My Own Butt'"* and *Pounded In The Butt By My Book "Pounded In The Butt By My Book 'Pounded In The Butt By My Book "Pounded In The Butt By My Own Butt""*" have all formed a long anal chain, moaning loudly as they enter each other.

To my left, *Anal Lesbian Pterodactyl Rodeo* and *My Librarian Is A Beautiful Lesbian Ice Cream Cone And She Tastes Amazing* are entangled on the boardroom table, eating each other out while *Dang, That's A Pretty Sweet Car That Just Ate My Butt* watches intently.

"Focus," *Sentient Bisexual Ketchup And Mustard Get Me Off* coos into my ear, drawing my attention back to her.

She reaches down and grabs hold of my stiff cock, aligning me with her wet entrance and then allowing me to thrust forward in a deep, powerful swoop.

The living book lets out a long sigh of pleasure as the two of us begin to move together, bucking in unison as we swiftly fall into sync. Wonderful sensations blossom across our bodies as we pick up speed, and soon enough we're slamming away with everything we've got.

Suddenly, I feel a tap on my shoulder. I slow down and look back to find *Bisexual Polyhedral Role-Playing Dice Orgy* standing behind me, his enormous dick at full attention. He doesn't have to say a word, because I know exactly what he's after.

"Do it," I command.

The living book aligns his rod with my tightly puckered backdoor and then firmly enters me, stretching the limits of my anal sphincter as he dives deep within. The sense of fullness is amazing, and although there's a brief moment of discomfort at the beginning, it quickly falls away as *Bisexual Polyhedral Role-Playing Dice Orgy* begins to move.

Of course, I'm still firmly planted within *Sentient Bisexual Ketchup And Mustard Get Me Off,* and eventually all three of us fall into a perfect, polyrhythmic groove together.

The feeling of being sandwiched between these incredible books is unlike anything I've ever experienced, and it's not long before the sensation begins to transform into the first hints of an impending orgasm.

"Oh my god, oh my god," I begin to repeat over and over again, the words growing louder and louder with every round of the frantic mantra until I'm screaming them out at the top of my lungs.

The whole broad room begins to chime in with cries of their own, edging closer and closer to a collective simultaneous orgasm.

I realize, of course, this perfectly timed climax would be quite difficult outside the confines of a book, but by now I'm satisfied with my place as the main character within my own story. We're here to prove love is real, after all, even between a human and the physical manifestation of the absurd volume of Chuck Tingle's literary catalog.

The orgasm hits me like a tidal wave, causing me to aburptly pull out of *Sentient Bisexual Ketchup And Mustard Get Me Off* and blast my spunk across her stomach. Meanwhile, the book up my ass thrusts deep and hold, his cum spilling out within me and filling my butthole until there's simply no room left. The next thing I know, his hot white jizz is squirting out from my anal edges and running down my legs in long, pearly streaks.

The whole boardroom is screaming with pleasure around us, cumming hard.

As the story comes to an end I feel inspired by the fact that Chuck Tingle has found an audience for this tale, as unique as it is. If there are readers out there who enjoy this, then there are certainly readers who will enjoy mine.

All I need to do is write with love, and start that first page.

SENTIENT BISEXUAL TENNIS BALLS PLAY MIXED DOUBLES IN MY BUTT

I've always been something of an athlete, enjoying every part of my workouts but particularly relishing the fun of competitive sport. There's just something about pushing myself to the next level that I find particularly exhilarating.

I played a lot of soccer when I was younger, and to be honest I think I got pretty good at it. I probably could've turned this passion into a career in the Women's Soccer League, but at a certain point I found myself getting frustrated. My competitive drive made the *team* aspect of soccer fairly unappealing. I didn't like the fact I could train ten times harder than anyone else on my squad, and at the end of the day it just didn't matter because I was one little cog in the big slow machine.

That's when I discovered tennis.

The sport of tennis is much different than anything else I'd played before, and for one distinct reason: it's not a team sport. In this game, all the training that I do will directly affect the outcome of my own games. If I lose, I know exactly who to blame.

Now that I've gotten older and worked my ass off, I feel like I've found myself with a truly commanding presence on the court. I can see all the angles and I know all the techniques. If I can imagine hitting the ball somewhere then I can almost always produce an equal result in real life, making the competition that I face more of a mental game than a physical one. To win at this level, you need to be more than just faster or stronger than the other players, you need to be smarter.

With all this said, however, I still have a long way to go. I've started entering competitions and doing fairly well, but I'm certainly not placing the way that I'd like to. I want to win, and this drive within me isn't slowing down. In fact, it's speeding up.

These days, it feels like I'm pushing up against a wall that's refusing to give. I keep practicing with my trainer and teacher, but even *she* seems to be growing frustrated. That's why I'm particularly nervous when I show up to the courts this afternoon. I've got the distinct impression that my trainer is going to deliver some bad news, but I'm not sure what it is.

Instead of paying for some fancy tennis courts, we use the local park. I don't think I could ever forgive myself if I started hanging around with those uptight county club types.

As I round the corner, I see that my trainer is waiting for me. Typically, she's already be out there slamming some tennis balls, but today she's sitting on a bench nearby. Clearly, something is up.

"Hi Amanda," I offer, waving as I approach and then sitting down next to her. "What's up?"

My trainer lets out a long sigh. "I'm sorry, but I've gotta be honest with you," she starts.

"I wouldn't ask for anything less," I continue. "You know I'm here to be the best I can be."

"That's the thing," Amanda counters. "I shouldn't be saying this, because I rely on these lessons for cash, but honestly you've… outgrown me."

Of all the things I'd been suspicious of, this was not one of them. My trainer's revelation takes me completely by surprise. "What do you mean?" I question. "I *love* coming here and working with you. That's how I got so good at tennis in the first place!"

"I know, I know," Amanda continues. "I love working with you, too. The problem is, I've got nothing left to teach. You're way better than me now, so it seems a little strange for me to critique your form. If you wanna hit some balls around then I'm happy to play, but I just don't feel right about acting like I'm your teacher anymore."

The sad gravity of this situation finally hits me. This is not an uncommon occurrence, as students outgrow their teachers all the time, but I suppose I'd imagined this would never happen between Amanda and me. She's my friend, after all, and part of what I like so much about this game is the fact that we get to spend our days out here in the park having fun.

Finally, I nod my head in acceptance. "I understand," I reply.

"It's been really great working with you, Wendy," my former trainer offers.

"Thanks. You too," I sigh, then open my arms and embrace my friend in a powerful hug.

We let out all of our emotion in this moment, purging it from our systems so that when we pull back again we can collect ourselves accordingly.

"So what now?" I question. "What am I gonna do to get better? Do I need to find a better trainer?"

"Kinda," Amanda replies. "Here's my advice: you need better gear."

I can't help but scoff at this. I've already invested plenty in the equipment I play with, so I can't imagine this being a legitimate solution.

"Trust me," Amanda continues, brushing away my skepticism. "I think you're ready. Go to the sports mart and ask for Pro Pounder 2000 High Impact Training Balls."

My friend hands me a piece of paper with these words scribbled across it in case I forget.

I raise an eyebrow, reading the brand back to myself in silence. "And you think this will work?" I question.

Amanda nods. "It's the next step."

I thank my friend and then stand up, deciding to walk to the sporting goods store from here. It's only a few blocks away, and most of that distance is on a nice trail that winds directly through the park.

We part ways and soon enough I find myself alone once more, strolling along as the sun peeks down between the branches above. There are others enjoying the park, having picnics to my left and playing basketball to my right, but at this moment I'm overwhelmed with a profound sense of solitude and loneliness. I was really looking forward to training with my friend today.

Of course, I've already spent this morning telling you about my resistance to team sports, but right now I kinda wish I wasn't the only one going through this particular challenge.

Eventually, I exit the park and make my way up the street a bit, arriving at the sporting goods store. I stroll in and head up to the counter.

"Hi there," offers the woman who works here. "How can I help you?"

"I'm looking for some new tennis balls," I reply, then pull out the folded piece of paper and read it word for word so that I'm sure to get it right. "I need the Pro Pounder 2000 High Impact Training Balls."

The woman behind the counter nods. "Of course! We've got those in back. Are you looking for the *adult* training balls or the regular training balls?"

"What's the difference," I counter.

"The adult ones will offer to fuck you in a wild bisexual orgy," the woman replies, "the regular balls will-"

I cut her off. "I'll take the adult ones."

"Sounds good!" the woman replies, then turns around and heads off to retrieve them from the back.

Moments later she returns carrying an enormous plastic tube. It's similar to the three ball sets that I've seen before, only this container is enlarged about twenty or thirty times the typical size. The woman helping me can barely wrap her arms around it, moving slowly and wobbling from side to side until she finally leans it against the counter.

"That'll be five dollars and fifty cents," the woman informs me.

I hand over the cash and then wrap my arms around the container, having just as much trouble maneuvering this thing as she did. I half-carry, half-drag it out of the sporting good store, somehow managing to pull it down the street then finally getting fed up once I reach the edge of the park.

Maybe this will be easier to carry once I open them.

I drop the giant plastic container and let it simply topple over onto the ground, laying there in the grass as I walk around to the side with the cap. I grab ahold of the plastic edge and then pull as hard as I can, peeling it back until it eventually unseals would a loud, satisfying pop.

I tumble back onto the ground as three tennis balls roll to a stop next to me.

"Hey," one of them offers as I sit up. "I'm Greet. Thanks for hiring us."

"I'm Brad," another one of them chimes in.

"And I'm Martina," the last interjects.

"It's nice to meet you," I reply. "I'm Wendy."

"Where's the court?" Brad questions. "Let's get to work."

The enormous yellow tennis balls roll around a bit, searching the area and then finally returning to my side.

"No court," Martina observes.

"I didn't think I could drag the container all the way there," I admit.

The sentient tennis balls exchange knowing glances.

"I bet we could do it as a team," Greet offers. "Maybe that's the first lesson of the day. Even though tennis is a solo activity, it's okay to rely on others for your training and support."

"Not just tennis," Brad continues. "That's a good life lesson."

I consider their words, nodding along and trying to follow despite the fact they're all talking at an unusually quick pace. "I understand," I reply.

"Then lets go!" Martina offers cheerfully. "Want a ride?"

"Sure," I reply.

Suddenly, all three of the tennis balls have rolled around me, tapping my legs from behind and causing me to tumble over onto their round, fuzzy bodies. The next thing I know, I'm being carried along, my body somehow staying supported while the tennis balls rotate underneath. I can't help but laugh, unable to control my outburst of excitement as I find myself carried along in this thrilling and unexpected manner.

Not only is it fun, but this method of transportation is also quite efficient. The next thing I know, I glance up to see that we're approaching the tennis court, tumbling through the gate and ending up in the middle of the green acrylic rectangle. It's here that I jump back to my feet, smiling wide.

"That was a blast!" I offer.

"Let's get started," Martina interjects, all business. "I'd like to see where your current skill level is at. Play me and we'll determine what needs improvement."

I pull out my racket and hand an extra one to Martina, who rolls over to the opposite side of the net. Once we're both in position, I throw a small, non-sentient tennis ball into the air and hammer it over to Martina's side with a devastatingly powerful serve.

The second I make contact I know it's going exactly where I want, but that doesn't seem to matter. In the blink of an eye, Martina is already over there in perfect position, ready and waiting to slam the ball back to me. She does so like a laser beam, and I'm not at all prepared. I make a valent attempt to return her hit, but I miss it.

"Again!" Martina calls out.

Brad tosses me another non-living tennis ball and I make another serve to Martina, this time trying a slightly different approach. Again, I'm impressed with my own movement as I hammer the ball over onto Martina's side, but somehow she's even more ready than the last time.

Martina immediately smacks the little yellow ball back toward me, angling it in such a way that it's simply impossible to get.

"Again!" Martina calls out.

"Damn, you're really good," I stammer, my breath short as I struggle to get the words out. I can't remember the last time I was challenged like this outside an official tournament. "Are you *all* this good?"

Brad rolls up to hand me another ball. "We are," he confirms.

I take a moment to catch my breath, centering myself before I make my third serve. I try my best to remember the importance of strategic placement, to consider where Martina thinks I'm going to hit the ball and then doing the exact opposite.

It doesn't work.

This time, Martina barely reacts, glancing over at Greet and Brad as she smacks my serve back and then strolls off the court. She doesn't even have to wait to see my attempt at a return.

I miss.

"Let's talk," the sentient tennis ball offers.

I stroll over to the three giant balls, wiping the sweat from my brow. My competitive nature has been awakened, but at this point I know there's no reason to get frustrated. These sentient tennis balls are so far beyond my skill level that I have nothing left to do but listen and learn.

We all meet on the edge of the court, forming a circle.

"What did you notice from the sidelines?" Martina asks her round friends.

"Not loose enough," Greet replies. "She's all wound up."

"Agreed," chimes in Brad.

Martina nods. "That's what I thought," the sentient sporting good replies, then turns her attention to me. "Listen, you've got some incredible physical skills, but right now your mental game is killing you. You're way too stressed."

"I am?" I question. "I don't feel stressed, I feel competitive."

"Whatever it is, you're tense," Martina continues. "It's inhibiting your swing and slowing your reaction time."

"Okay," I confirm with a nod. "What should I do about it?"

"Well, there are two options," the sentient tennis ball replies. "The slow option is we could send you on a vacation with plenty of spa days and massages and some time out on the beach."

"That sounds like heaven," I reply. "What's the other option?"

"The fast way, where we have a hardcore bisexual orgy wi-"

"The fast way," I blurt. "I'll take that one."

"I haven't even finished explaining," Martina begins, but I'm already taking off my clothes.

The sentient tennis balls exchange glances, then shrug as they roll closer and surround my body.

The next thing I know, all three of the gorgeous balls are massaging my form, running their hands up and down my frame as we explore one another excitedly. In an effort to cover as much vertical area as possible, my lovers roll up on top of one another, stacked like a snowman as they continue to tease me.

Of course, the one at my waist still takes his time, running his hands along my hips but not going any farther as I continue to strip down. Up top, Martina is kissing me passionately on the lips, making out with me while I allow myself to melt.

I'm realizing now just how correct this sentient collection of sporting goods is. My competitive nature is great in some regards, but it's also keeping me in a perpetual state of tension. I'm constantly thinking about what I need to accomplish instead of what I already have, but right now it's difficult to imagine how the present could get any better.

"That feels so good," I gush.

"Fuck yeah," offers Greet from down below as he caresses my legs and calves.

At this point, Brad begins to move his hands closer and closer to my most sensitive areas, his fingers drifting closer and closer and then pulling back at the last second. He's doing this on purpose, making me ache for more and taking his time with me.

"Please," I coo. "Do it."

Martina pulls back a bit. "Do what?" she questions.

"Oh," I stammer. "I was taking to Brad. All three of you standing on top of each other is very confusing."

"We can just float if you'd like," Martina offers.

The next thing I know, all of the tennis balls stop what they're doing and hover up to eye level.

"You can float!" I blurt. "Why did you wait until just now?"

"We try not to hover very often," Greet explains. "You can't really have a floating tennis ball anywhere near the courts, that's cheating, so we use this ability sparingly."

"If you'd like we can carry you around above the clouds, seeing the sights on a magical journey," Brad continues, "or we can just get back to the bisexual org-"

"Get back to the bisexual orgy," I interject. "Let's go!"

I seize the moment, kissing Martina passionately on the lips and pushing her back so that, soon enough, we've arrived against the chain link fence that surrounds the court. The rest of the tennis balls follow closely behind and now I'm kissing all of them, moving from one to the next in a fit of passion.

I'd been so focused on Martina that I'd barely noticed the guys, but now that I have a chance to kiss each of them I can sense the erotic tension building even more. This is going to be a good time.

It's not long before Brad gets back to work down below. Instead of continuing to tease me with his hands, the sentient orb floats low and runs his finger across my aching clit, slowly rubbing me as a soft moan escapes from between my lips. I close my eyes tight and lean my head back, reveling in this wonderful moment and allowing myself to give in completely.

I begin to rock my hips against the movement of the tennis ball, the two of us falling into sync with one another as he keeps a steady pace. Eventually, Brad opens his mouth and dives in, lapping away at me with his tongue. He only gets a few licks in before Martina floats down into position, pushing the tennis ball away and picking up right where Brad left off.

"No need to fight," I laugh. "There's plenty to go around."

Encouraged by my words, Greet and Brad hover back up to eye level, an enormous cock now protruding from each one of their bodies. They jut out toward me with impressive girth, two giant shafts at the ready.

I take one in each hand and begin to pump my fingers across their length, beating off the tennis balls while Martina continues to eat me out down below. The sensation of being at the center of all this is incredible, and I don't hesitate for a moment as I open my mouth and take Brad's swollen cock within.

I pump my face up and down across the living tennis ball's shaft a few times before popping him out of my mouth and replacing him with Greet's massive rod. I continue like this for a good while and then finally decide to take them both at the same time, holding their dicks together while I somehow manage to fit them both between my lips.

The bisexual tennis balls clearly enjoy this, not just the sensation of my tongue massaging their shafts, but also the fact their dicks are pressed together so firmly. I watch as they begin to passionately make out with one another, lost in this erotic moment.

Down below, Martina has moved on from the long drags of her tongue. She's much more focused now, rapidly moving this wet muscle back and forth across my clit and causing tremors of passion to flood my body. I can feel the first hint of a powerful orgasm building up within me, these feelings blooming in the pit of my stomach and then working their way out across my arms and legs.

I begin to moan loudly into the cocks that fill my mouth, pushing steadily closer to my impending orgasm. Martina slips two fingers within me and begins to add this new movement to the sensual polyrhythm of our bodies.

Finally, I just can't take it anymore, releasing the cocks from my mouth and throwing my head back in a state of unbridled passion. I scream wildly, my voice carrying out across the tennis courts as the muscles of my stomach clench tight and then release in a spastic fit. Meanwhile, Martina doesn't let up for a second, keeping the pace as I cum harder than I ever have.

When I finally finish I stumble a bit, eventually collapsing to the green acrylic in a panting heap.

I should be utterly spent, but somehow this orgasm has done the exact opposite. Instead of tiring me out, the carnal explosion has kicked me into overdrive. I want more.

I crawl across the tennis court a bit, popping my bare rump out at the sentient tennis balls seductively. "Fuck me!" I command.

Immediately, the round living objects spring into action, each one of them knowing exactly how to position themselves. Martina rolls over to the front and starts by kissing me on the lips, then eventually guides my face lower and lower across her body. Soon enough, I've reached her pussy, which I don't hesitate to dive in on. I begin to lap away at her, eating her out with just as much enthusiasm as she'd provided to me just moments earlier.

As I work Martina orally, I can feel one of the tennis balls rolling into position under my body. I lift myself up so he can get fully underneath and properly align himself, then moments later I feel the sweet fullness of his enormous tennis ball cock sliding into my pussy. I let out a long, satisfied groan as Greet enters me, enjoying the way he holds firm as I adjust to the tennis ball's incredible side.

Eventually, Greet begins to pump in and out of my body, the two of us gradually falling into sync with one another as we steadily rock.

"Oh fuck, oh fuck, oh fuck," I repeat over and over again, mumbling the words into Martina's pussy as I continue to eat her out. My volume builds as I repeat these words over and over again, until eventually I'm screaming at the top of my lungs.

Still, I want more. I pull away from Martina just long enough to glance back over my shoulder and make eye contact with Brad. "What are you waiting for?" I snarl, reaching around and giving my ass a firm slap. "Get in there."

The sentient tennis ball floats down into position behind me, aligning his cock with my puckered back door while Greet continues to thrust from the front. He takes a moment to position himself, then finally thrusts forward, impaling me across his length.

I let out a frantic howl, utterly beside myself with pleasure as the tennis balls hammer away at me in a rowdy double penetration. When one of them pulls out, the other pushes in, back and forth like this as the two of them gradually pick up speed.

The sensation is unlike anything I've ever felt, and I have to admit it takes me a moment to get used to. I'm so full that it feels like some kind of discomfort is warranted, but that sensation never comes. Instead, I find my body relaxing, falling into a state of blissed out flow.

When I finally collect myself I return to eating out Martina, and soon enough all four of us begin to loudly moan. We've somehow all fallen into a perfectly timed set of movements, our bodies sliding against one another in a way that I would've never expected.

We're working as a team.

"Oh my god!" I suddenly blurt. "I'm gonna cum again!"

"Fuck yes!" Martina shrieks, preparing for an orgasm of her own.

The tennis ball before me throws her head back as I carry her across the finish line, lost in a moment of erotic bliss. Meanwhile, Brad thrusts deep into my ass and holds, expelling a blast of his hot white spunk. I cum along with him, and soon enough all three of us are moaning in a chorus of pleasure.

The tennis ball below me comes soon after, pulling his cock out of my pussy and then allowing Brad to float down and suck him off. The other sentient object only gets three pumps in before Greet is blowing his spunk in a forceful payload. Brad swallows hungrily, then drops to the ground with the rest of us is a state of utter exhaustion.

Just then I notice a man and woman watching us from the edge of the tennis court. They both wear a look of deep concern across their faces.

"We're almost done!" I call out to them. "Sorry about that!"

The couple walks away just shaking their heads.

"That was amazing," I gush to the tennis balls that surround me. "What a great first lesson."

I still like to play solo, but strangely that's not my favorite method of competing anymore. I'm placing pretty high in my tournaments now, thanks to the help and training of my new living object team, but the game of one on one tennis just isn't where my heart is.

Now, I'm receiving a first place trophy, but only *half* of it belongs to me.

I glance over at Amanda, my former teacher and now teammate, who stands on the podium next to me. It's not a ten person team, but playing doubles is *much more* than I was originally comfortable with.

It looks like keeping an open mind was worth it.

Amanda and me gaze out over the crowd of onlookers as they applaud esthetically. Brad, Greet and Martina are floating in the front row, smiling wide, and I feel more relaxed than I have in a very long time.

ABOUT THE AUTHOR

Dr. Chuck Tingle is an erotic author and Tae Kwon Do grandmaster (almost black belt) from Billings, Montana. After receiving his PhD at DeVry University in holistic massage, Chuck found himself fascinated by all things sensual, leading to his creation of the "tingler", a story so blissfully erotic that it cannot be experienced without eliciting a sharp tingle down the spine. Chuck's hobbies include backpacking, checkers and sport.

CPSIA information can be obtained
at www.ICGtesting.com
Printed in the USA
FSHW020559280721
83624FS